BRAVER THAN
THE GURKHAS

BRAVER THAN THE GURKHAS

Sikhar

WORD PUBLISHING

WORD (UK) Ltd
Milton Keynes, England

WORD AUSTRALIA
Heathmont, Victoria, Australia

WORD COMMUNICATIONS LTD
Vancouver, B.C., Canada

STRUIK CHRISTIAN BOOKS (PTY) LTD
Maitland, South Africa

ALBY COMMERCIAL ENTERPRISES PTE LTD
Balmoral Road, Singapore

CHRISTIAN MARKETING NEW ZEALAND LTD
Havelock North, New Zealand

JENSCO LTD
Hong Kong

SALVATION BOOK CENTRE
Malaysia

BRAVER THAN THE GURKHAS

ISBN 0-85009-345-7 (Australia ISBN 1-86258-095-2) (STL ISBN 1-85078-080-3)

Printed in England by Clays Ltd, St Ives plc

STL books are published by Send The Light (Operation Mobilisation), PO Box 48, Bromley, Kent, England.

90 91 92 93 / 10 9 8 7 6 5 4 3 2 1

In Memory of

Bir Bahadur Rai

the first known Nepali martyr for 'Yesu'

FOREWORD

In 1987 along with David Atkinson, the M.P. for Bourne-mouth, I travelled over one thousand miles within Nepal taking evidence from the country's beleaguered Christians. The facts which we gathered into a stark report closely mirror the story which you are about to read. For 'Braver than the Gurkhas' is not a fantasy tale of make-believe. It is an elegant portrayal of life for any Christian convert in Nepal. It graphically and truthfully charts the brutal repression which awaits all who embrace the Christian message.

The story reminds me of our first reactions on meeting Nepali Christians. Here I felt in direct contact with the church of Acts, the Pentecostal church. Low on possessions, sharing what is available, meeting in makeshift buildings, suffering persecution, vilification, and abuse. Here is the church in all its persecuted purity untainted by the effects of western materialism and clear in its values and teachings. Here are Christians willing to risk six years in jail for their faith. Here are women – so reminiscent of the faithful women of the New Testament – steadfastly carrying the burden of cruelty and separation from jailed loved ones. Here are men prepared to face the brutality of police beatings and time in medieval stocks.

Among the Nepali Christians I met was Sikhar – a name with an appropriate double meaning. Said short it means 'summit'; said long it means 'victim'. A country which boasts Everest and the Himalayan mountains has no shortages of summits nor, more sadly and less picturesque, of victims. He has used his own unique insights to weave this story of courage and patient endurance.

How often you will be reminded of Paul and his early persecution of the believers; of his subsequent conversion and his own Christian rebirth. You will be reminded of Jesus' warning that His teachings are not a cosy option but one which will drive wedges between families; one which will leave you reviled for His name. Sikhar cannot paint a picture of comfortable Christianity because in Nepal – the second poorest country – it does not exist. Instead it is a picture of humiliation, torture, poverty and love.

This book will be a milestone in raising awareness about the plight of Nepal's 25,000 Christians. It underlines the daily violation of Article 18 of the United Nations Declaration of Human Rights; the article which supposedly guarantees our right to change and follow our religion. But it is more than that. It is a beautifully written and inspirational book which should be required reading for all who place so little value on the freedoms we take so much for granted.

David Alton
Liverpool;
Member of Parliament for Liverpool, Mossley Hill;
Parliamentary Advisor to the Jubilee Campaign,
which works for Christian prisoners of conscience.

ACKNOWLEDGEMENTS

'Braver than the Gurkhas' has been a team-project. During my early days at word-processing, invaluable help was given by my fellow student Vernon Wilkins. My wife Shanti read the novel first, but was too biased to find any fault with it! Ray Porter, Clare Wenham, Dr Beryl Hawker, and Shirley Dobson all gave valuable suggestions. Dr and Mrs Bill Gould and Dr John Sleggs advised on medical and broader issues. Quite a few chapters were written in the homes of Bill and Pam Hampson and Drs Philip and Anne Simms who kindly invited us during the Christmas of 1987. Finally, the willingness of the Honourable David Alton M.P. – a dedicated Christian who has been to Nepal to study the situation first-hand – to provide an introduction was a tremendous encouragement. To all of you, hearty thanks!

The novel revolves around true events: the death of a Christian through police brutality, the arrest of a group of believers (including the author), and the Nepalese government's treatment of the Christian minority in general. I apologise in advance for some of the scenes which may prove to be offensive. I have kept them only because 'fact is stranger than fiction'. Though the characters portray the reality for native Christians in modern Nepal, they are still entirely fictional. Most of the words in italics are terms kept to give a distinctly Nepali flavour and are explained in the glossary at the end of this book.

Sikhar
May 1990

TABLE OF CONTENTS

HOW IT ALL STARTED

After centuries of isolation from the rest of the world and a hereditary dictatorship which lasted 104 years, Nepal finally became a democratic state in 1950. To bring this about, a lot of Nepali men had given their lives; women had suffered widowhood. For a while, it seemed the blood of the martyrs was not spilt in vain.

The interim Government of Nepal Act 1950, promulgated by King Tribhuvan, stated clearly: 'His Majesty's Government shall not discriminate against any citizen on grounds of religion, race, caste, sex, place of birth . . .' (Art 15, no. 1). The next constitution he offered was modelled on the secular constitutions of democracies like India. The untimely death of this king soon reversed the progress gained through earlier sacrifices. The brief taste of democracy enjoyed by Nepal was to be snatched away.

In 1960, his successor suspended the constitution, and two years later made Nepal a one-party, one-religion (Hindu) state. Political parties were banned, basic human rights denied. New laws decreed that any person who was converted to Christianity or Islam should be sentenced to at least a year in prison, and that anyone convicted of converting others should get six years. The anti-conversion laws and the absence of an opposition party to point out excesses has given this government the licence to exploit, torture, and abuse its citizens. This reign of terror, which suppresses anyone who dares think or act differently, has so far continued unchecked.

Recently Nepal, which has been called a 'rich country with poor people' by one of her most prominent citizens, has been rated the second poorest country in the world. Certainly, the all-round development and prosperity promised by her totalitarian regime has proved a mirage. After thirty years of this regime, not a single paved road links the eastern border with the west. Citizens with some financial means, despite their patriotic feelings for their country, have despaired and migrated elsewhere. Hundreds of others who dare to ask for reform, aged politicians as well as young students, languish in jail. Blood is being spilt again, this time to restore the short lived democracy won by the previous generation.

This is the background to the story you are about to read – the story of a father and daughter who dared to think and act differently.

CHAPTER
ONE

THE ASSAULT

Mother was crying. Renu knew she had heard a sob from inside the house. She stopped scrubbing the pot which Mother had used for cooking the rice. She left it next to the pit at the eastern end of the courtyard; and with the black straw scrubber still in her right hand, she bent to enter the narrow door.

Mother had not stopped doing her chores. In the pale yellow light of the kerosine lamp, she was applying ochre paste to the floor around the fire-place. With the back of her left hand, Mother wiped her eyes, completely oblivious that Renu had entered.

'What's the matter, Mother?' Renu asked.

'Oh!' replied Sanumaya, 'I thought you were scrubbing the pots outside.'

'Has Father bothered you again?' Renu suggested.

Sanumaya's frequent sobs interrupted the story, but finally Renu got the gist of it. Father had drunk too much again. He regularly came home and beat Sanumaya while Renu, helpless to do anything, would cringe and watch. That evening events had taken a disastrous turn. He had beaten up *Patrus Masih*.

Patrus Masih came from a city that Renu had always wanted to visit – Darjeeling. In fact it was the stories that Patrus had told her in class the year before that had aroused in her the desire to go there. When the British ruled India, they transformed this mountainous village across the eastern border of Nepal into a beautiful hill station. Patrus had remarked how clean the British had kept it. 'It's grown a lot dirtier now, but nothing like the bus station in Kathmandu. That looks like a paddy field: you can grow rice there!' How Renu wanted to see Darjeeling! However, she was not in the mood to play the tourist just then. Patrus had brought *Yesu*, the Christian God, to the village. She hated him for it.

'Father has beaten up Patrus Masih,' Sanumaya said. 'Renu, where will we go? Soon the police will be after him. They'll take him away. Then I'll live like a widow . . .' The thought proved too much for her. She took the tip of her *fariah*, and blew her nose into it.

'Perhaps, the police won't come,' Renu tried to console her, still standing and holding the dirty black scrubber in her hand. 'The Christians usually just pray about everything to their *Yesu*.'

'Not this time. Mane has gone to report the matter,' Sanumaya assured her daughter. 'Sanat told me. He is one of our few friends in the village. Most others have turned Christian.'

'Shh, I can hear Father coming,' whispered Renu. 'I'll get to the pots.' Renu stole away to the scrubbing pit like a cat refused a place next to the fire.

The master of the house, Mahila, arrived seconds later. He staggered to the wooden pillar that supported the thatch roof over the verandah and embraced it.

'Sanu,' he croaked. Sanumaya peered into the smoky blue room, through the door, to the shiny, sweaty face framed in the rectangular light patch of the kerosine lamp.

'*Ram, Ram!*' she muttered to herself. 'He has surely had plenty of liquor tonight!'

Sanumaya did not have to reply to Mahila. She kept on watching in horror as he loosened his embrace. A piece of firewood in his right hand trembled as he swayed a step onto the verandah. He could not complete the next step, but slumped to the straw mat. His eyes stared into the night, across the Trisuli river.

'I had to do it, I had to do it!' he muttered through clenched teeth. A few seconds later, Sanumaya heard him snore, and guessed that the local brew had gone to his head.

'Renu,' she called. Renu preferred to keep her distance when Father got home drunk.

'Yes, Mother, I'll put the pots inside and come.'

When Renu reached her mother, she found her trying to open Mahila's fist that clenched the piece of wood. With some moans, Mahila let it go.

'Bring the blanket, cover him well, there's no way we can

carry him upstairs,' Sanumaya said in one breath. The wooden ladder creaked as Renu went up. Each plank produced a different tone. She returned with the blanket a few minutes later.

'Renu, look, blood on the wood! *Ram, Ram*, what shall we do?' Sanumaya looked at her daughter.

'I know what I'll do – I'll put it into the fire,' Renu replied. Snatching away the shivering faggot from Mother's hand, she went to the fire-place, an ash-filled hole with a metal tripod in the centre of the ground floor. The red embers were coated with grey. Renu shoved the bloody end of the wood into the embers, threw a few twigs on top, and blew gently. A hesitant flame soon appeared. She nursed it till it burned brightly.

'Take Father's dinner off the tripod', Sanumaya warned her. Renu hastily caught the handle of the pot, lifted it off the tripod, and let it rest on the ashes away from the flame.

'Good thing we ate before he came,' Sanumaya added. 'I couldn't have swallowed a mouthful after the smell of this horrid stuff he has drunk.'

'It makes me so sad.' Renu had to say something. 'You or I don't matter to him at all. All he wants is liquor. It's a good thing flies don't come at night. Otherwise, they'd be swarming around his face by now.' Half of the wood had already turned into charcoal.

'Shut the door and come up, Renu. We have a lot to do tomorrow.' Renu pushed the wooden bolt from one flank of the door into the other. She thought for a while, and undid the bolt. Father would probably want to come in when the drink left him.

Renu lay on her bed and stared at the ceiling above her. She had heard that her grandfather had built the house that she, Father, and Mother lived in. Probably it was thirty years old, but in arguments Renu had doubled the age to impress her friends. During the previous year, she had seen hired workmen replace the sooty straw that had served as the roof till then. She had never seen her grandfather, but heard stories that most of the stones that formed the wall of the house came from the cliffs of Tarachuli hill against which her village nestled. Mud glued one stone to the other. On the outside, Renu could see how rain and wind had eaten deep crevices between the stones. Inside, the plaster which was daubed with a mixture of cow dung and red clay formed fairly even surfaces. Mud floor, mud plaster, mud mortar! The door and window frames, neither varnished nor painted but daubed with ochre, looked like mud too. In reality, these frames and panes came from the gradually decreasing pine forest at the summit of Tarachuli. Worms had eaten countless holes in them, depositing white powder on the floor, but Renu did not mind. The house would outlast her as it had her grandfather.

Then her thoughts turned to her father. Renu could remember the Great War stories he had told her from the time she was nine. His heroism, his devotion to the goddess Kali made her blood boil. His military career had given him an extraordinary gift. He could read and write faster than lightning! Father had casually attributed his skill to the endless reports he had to prepare for his superior officers. Renu had loved receiving his letters from Kathmandu when Father had gone there on business. He did not drink then, and those were the good old days. She was not sure whether he loved her as much now. At fifteen, she could no longer sit on his lap; but her love for her father, at least when sober, did not fade.

She could not condone the beating of this Christian preacher, but she understood what inspired Father to do it.

'Not a single Christian four years ago in Dhanee Gaon, now over forty! We have to stop this,' Father had muttered many times. His Great War had yet to finish.

If anyone could stop the rise of Christians, Father thought he could. He felt sure his religion surpassed all others. He had fought the Japanese in Burma. To get courage for the war, he had torn off the border of his mother's *fariah* and worn it as a sacred thread around his neck and under his right arm. He had taken a small picture of the goddess Kali in the left pocket of his under-garment. He believed the goddess Kali made him invisible to the Japanese. When a sniper almost got him in the Naga hills, uttering a prayer to Kali, he dived flat to the ground. No more bullets! Kali had saved him. Mother Kali could drive the Christians out of Dhanee Gaon too. Hadn't she chosen him for the task?

Mother kept herself occupied. She had taken the kerosine lamp to the top floor. Renu climbed up, and saw Mother sitting

18

up in her wooden cot, leaning against the wall, her pillow behind her back. Mother's head bent downward, her lips moved silently. Underneath the sooty, yellow quilt, her hand must have been operating the prayer-beads: Renu saw the quilt move in a strange rhythm. She knew Mother was invoking *Ram's* help again.

Sanumaya did not mind distractions, even in prayer.

'Mother, how did my teacher come to our village in the first place?'

'You mean that thief from Darjeeling!' Sanumaya retorted, ceasing her prayers as easily as she had begun. 'He came at a time when they didn't have anyone to teach English at the school. The village was keen to welcome the English teacher and his wife to the school, wasn't it? The dumb Tamangs were glad to have their children learn from him. Many passed the tests for the first time. But, Patrus Masih was too cunning for them. No one suspected him. Rane Subbha went over as the first *Yesu* follower. The Jogbir family followed. Karna hesitated a bit, but joined the band as well. Now after just four years, about forty people gather every Saturday to sing and pray to *Yesu*.'

'Is that why Father pulled me out of school?' Renu slid herself into her bed.

'That's one reason,' Sanumaya replied. 'Money doesn't come easily to a drunkard. He has only his pension and the sale of crops to go on. The rains failed us last year. That meant less money for him. He has behaved very badly.'

Renu did not know what to say. She looked pathetically at her mother for a while – the usual lonely figure in a bed meant for two. The constant beatings from her drunken husband and the unceasing anxiety to keep the family fed had slimmed Mother considerably.

What prospects did marriage have for my mother? Renu could not help thinking. What'll it have for me?

Mother broke the uneasy silence. 'We'd better save kerosine. Turn off the lamp, will you?' Renu stretched her neck out and blew onto the lamp, too hard. Half a breath would have sufficed. Mother always kept the wick low to conserve the precious oil. Renu tried to sleep. When her eyes got used to the darkness, she saw Mother's figure again, calling, '*Ram, Ram.*'

She wants to fight sleep, Renu pitied her mother; she should sleep and forget the troubles for a while. A frog croaking far away punctuated the silence.

Renu dreamed that dogs were barking ferociously. She tried to placate them by throwing pieces of millet bread at them. That did not work. The dogs swallowed the bread, and continued chasing her all the same. They chased her to the edge of a cliff. She had to make a decision fast. Either let the dogs tear her up or jump into the Trisuli river below! She uttered 'Ram, Ram' and jumped into the churning water.

'What's the matter?'

Renu could not believe her ears. Had Father crawled up the ladder into his place beside Mother? Had the drink lost its effect? It evidently had. Mother was no longer sitting up. Renu saw her sleeping properly.

'I heard dogs barking,' Renu replied. 'What a horrible dream. I must have screamed.'

'Not a dream, *nani*,' Mahila corrected. 'The dogs have never barked louder.' When sober, Father sounded like an angel.

Mother stirred, wriggled, and sat up. Mahila had already gone to the wooden window frame that lay between Renu's bed and his. He peered through it.

'Dogs are barking, but I don't see anyone. What's this?' he muttered. Renu saw him stare through the cracks between the wooden panes.

'Dogs bark if they've smelled a fox.' Sanumaya knew this from experience. 'Get back to bed.'

'What do I see?' exclaimed Mahila. 'Two people walking our way!'

'They must be going to the next village,' Sanumaya replied.

'You fool, the way to the next village doesn't pass through our courtyard. The men are coming to our home!'

'Relatives?' Sanumaya suggested.

'Your relatives, idiot, the police!' Mahila's military self returned to him. He felt for the key on a string around Sanumaya's neck. 'Quick, money,' he said.

Sanumaya did not protest. She fumbled at the string and took it out. Mahila grabbed it, and rushed to the wooden chest at the foot of the cot.

Renu had heard the mumbled conversation of the newcomers down below. Serves him right, she thought. Soon she corrected herself: *Ram, Ram,* make the police go away.

Ex-Sergeant Mahila had to rely heavily on his military craftiness. He reckoned it best to meet the police, and call them in for a chat before they called him out. He had taken what he wanted from the wooden chest. He shut the lid gently, and slid down the wooden ladder.

Renu went to Sanumaya's bed, and huddled together with her under the quilt.

'They'll take Father,' Sanumaya whispered.

Renu pictured the two policemen with rifles escorting Mahila away. She heard their boots squeak 'churm, churm' on the rocky track.

Renu slid to the window pane, and pressed her eyes against it. Father must've lied again, she thought. She saw two men with black Nepali caps, trousers and green canvas boots. The men looked as puzzled as her Father had seemed a few minutes ago. Unable to shout for Mahila because of the dogs barking around them, they stared up at the roof, down to the door, and up again. They must have heard the door open. The men walked towards it.

Renu could not bear the suspense. She did not want to watch any further. Going to her mother's bed, she huddled up to her again. Most of the dogs had run out of breath, but one kept on whining. Another joined it now and then. Father must have been gone for fifteen minutes. To Renu the time seemed an eternity.

'*Ram, Ram,* save us from this disgrace,' Sanumaya sighed aloud. Renu heard the door close, the ladder creak. The twilight through the joints of the wooden window pane revealed her Father's half smile as he appeared on the top rung of the ladder.

'They've gone,' Mahila said. 'I'll go too in a few minutes!'

'What! Who?' Sanumaya enquired.

'The police, you fool!'

'But Renu says they didn't look like police!'

'Police in civilian clothes,' Mahila explained. 'They have more brains than you. They didn't want the other villagers to know.'

'But where will you go?' Sanumaya felt she had a right to

find out.

'They agreed not to arrest me. They told me to vanish for a few days. I'll return on Monday afternoon. If anyone asks for me, tell them I've gone to Kathmandu on business.'

Sanumaya kept quiet. Renu felt she did the wise thing. Arguments with Father only made matters worse. From the cradle to the funeral pyre, the Nepalese woman must remain quiet!

Mahila fumbled as he hurried in the dark. Renu saw him sling on the shoulder bag. The ladder creaked, the door opened softly. The dogs stopped barking as they saw the familiar figure of Mahila emerge. Renu heard the 'flip-flop, flip-flop' of the thonged sandals Mahila wore, loud at first, then faint, then no more. Father had disappeared like this many times before, but always to cut firewood or get drunk. The reason for the disappearance that morning made Renu shudder.

Sanumaya crawled along the bed to the wooden chest. Her money pouch lay thrown carelessly on top of the bedclothes. Taking the pouch to the twilight of the window, she pulled at the two strings to open it.

'Only fifty rupees left,' she moaned.

'How much did you have, Mother?'

'Three hundred and fifty.' Sanumaya squatted motionless on the floor. 'How shall I manage the fields now?'

CHAPTER
TWO

THE CHILD EATER

Sometimes she considered herself fortunate, sometimes not. Being the only child has advantages as well as disadvantages. Renu did not have anyone to whom she could pour out her heart.

After Father had disappeared, Renu had done her share of fetching water from the village tap at the bottom of the bamboo thicket. She went back and forth three times with the brass water vessel balanced on her left hip. This supply lasted till the evening when she had to make two trips again.

After the morning rice meal, Renu untied the buffalo, the cow and the seven-month-old calf, and led them up the hill. Six months earlier and without the animals, she would have gone down towards her village school. Times had changed. Her ambition to finish high school and train as a nurse in Kathmandu had gone haywire. Like most other girls in the village, she knew exactly how the future would treat her. Till her parents found a husband for her, she would tend the cattle. Then she would have children (perhaps a few miscarriages like her mother), worry about feeding them and keeping the family together. If she got a drunkard for her husband, then beatings and bruises would mark her days. Till old age bent her down and her limbs stopped working, the buffaloes and cows would need her attention.

She decided to take them to a pasture she knew. It still had some grass left. Up, up, up and right! It meant a lot of walking for the cattle, but the grass they would get would compensate for that.

The ten o'clock *Falgun* sun tempted her to turn her back to it, and doze off. She knew the best place for this. The cattle had already reached it along the path before her, chosen a green patch each, and begun to graze. Seeing them content, she entered a plot separated by a row of wild raspberry bushes.

'Oh,' she gasped, 'a man already sleeping there!' She was about to turn back when she noticed the cloth shoulder bag on which he laid his head. It looked familiar, as did the person asleep.

'Father!' she called out the moment she recognised him. Mahila woke up startled. His right hand reached out instinctively to the item under his head. Only then did he look up at his daughter.

'Renu!' he said, yawning and rubbing his eyes, 'you've found me!'

'I didn't come looking for you,' Renu replied. 'I decided to bring the cattle further up today. We don't have much grass left elsewhere.'

'The winter rains haven't come as they should. Last year the monsoon failed us,' Mahila added. 'We may have a famine. . . Have you had your rice?' The gentle manner of the question took her completely by surprise.

'Have you had anything to eat?' she asked.

'No! I didn't dare go to the tea shop at the Tarachuli summit. Someone there could report me to the police. I decided not to run away. Where can I go? The police-thugs managed to extort two hundred rupees out of me. I felt too depressed for fast walking. I could've gone to your mother's family home, but they'd hate to see a drunkard like me. I smoked two cigarettes while going to the toilet this morning.'

'How can you do it? Smoke, and go to the toilet at the same time?' Renu looked repulsed by the very thought.

'Once you make a habit of it, it comes quite easily,' Mahila added as jovially as he could. 'Nothing like the cigarette fumes to cleanse your bowels. I smoked another waiting for the sun to come out. Then I must've fallen asleep till now.'

'Father, if you don't run away, what'll you do?' Renu sat beside him.

'I'll finish the work I've begun,' Mahila replied.

'You mean you'll beat up more Christians?' Renu guessed. 'Why don't you leave the Christians alone? You smashed up Patrus Masih. Haven't you had enough?'

'Shh, Renu, you don't understand. Four years ago, not a

single Christian in the village! Now scores of them. Someone has to do something.'

'Who made you that "someone"? Just because you served as a sergeant in the army long ago, you don't have any right to assume the position of the village guard. Your drunken bouts have already lost you your reputation.' Renu did not realise she was almost shouting.

'Let me tell you something – the police are also planning to drive the Christians out of the village,' Mahila said with a smile. Suddenly more interested, Renu drew closer.

'Just after leaving home this morning, I changed my mind about running away immediately. Instead of heading upwards to the Tarachuli summit, I decided to go towards the village tap to take care of nature first and then wash my face. I happened to look downhill towards the Trisuli valley. I saw two lights shining and then going hazy at a distance. I felt puzzled, and wondered if I was seeing the eyes on the chest of the female headless monster. Villagers said one roamed about in the forest. I decided to go closer to get a better view. Washing my face could wait.

'The lights moved a bit in the air, but apparently remained at the same distance. I took the path as long as I could. A few minutes later, I realised the lights did not belong to a headless monster after all. When I could distinguish who held the lights, I recognised the policemen who had just extorted two hundred rupees out of me. I jumped for cover behind a bush.

'I guessed the policemen had stopped to light the cigarettes they hadn't been able to smoke at our home. For a while, I felt my heart breathe fast. They must be discussing whom to plunder next, I thought. The one-hour walk along the Trisuli valley and the two-hour climb straight up to our home must have tired them out!

'I slid from one bush to another to get closer to the men. Evidently, the cigarettes they'd lit earlier were finished. The elder of the two asked his junior to light another. The fellow took out a crumpled packet of *Gainda*. I think there were about three cigarettes in it. He straightened them out, offered one to his superior, and, taking out his matches, lit it. Then the elder said that there was no need to report everything to Inspector Kuber Singh. They'd just say that the culprit had absconded. I immediately knew he was talking about me. Then the junior chattered away about the "big catch" they'd just taken, obviously referring to the money they managed to extort from me. The elder mentioned that there was a bigger catch yet to come.

"*Dasain* is months away, but we'd better start preparing for it right now. Do you want a big Indian goat for *Asthami*, Lal?" Then I caught the name of his junior. When Lal didn't get the point, the elder called him "son of a widow", and made him swear that he wouldn't divulge the plan.

"May I turn into a leper if I do so, Sub-Inspector sahib!" swore Lal. I laughed quietly. Only then did I know the rank of the elder one. The sub-inspector started talking about me again.

"We can't possibly squeeze much more out of Mahila. He's served in the army: he knows how to deal with us. He said he'd run away, but go to his home tonight and you'll find him under the quilt with his wife! Probably he's just hidden in the attic. But the man he beat up can help us." I laughed again. How would they get a bigger catch?

"The fellow who has the strange name of Patrus Masih came here from Darjeeling. Arrest him, and he'll pay anything to get out!" the sub-inspector explained. Then he began talking about the law. "The law promises prison sentences for making anyone a Christian. This fellow Patrus must have made scores. Just lock him up, and the fun begins. Rather than remain in jail, this fellow can throw a few thousands to us. All American money!"

'I saw Lal daydreaming. He came to himself only when his senior asked for his cigarette stub. Talking too much and smoking too little, the sub-inspector had extinguished his. When Lal expressed doubts about the inspector, his senior was confident. "The pighead will agree to anything I say. He knows the trade as we do. I must promise him something . . . Didn't you see the truck owner put in custody the other day? The son of a widow doesn't know that Kuber used his truck and driver the whole day. He transported sand to build the Trisuli goddess shrine at the sub-station you see below." Lal's superior pointed down to the tin-roofed structure just at the entrance to the suspension bridge across the river. The conversation grew more interesting. The sub-inspector complained bitterly that the rascal of an inspector didn't give him a single rupee. As if in anger, he stood up from the stone, wiped the dust off the seat of his trousers, and sat down again.

"The IGP sahib donated the money for the shrine," the sub-inspector added. "Perhaps he did it to atone for all the fish he dynamited in the Trisuli river." Then I got the point. Our government prohibits fishing like that. Probably, the inspector had provided the dynamite! So the IGP gave the money as much to keep the inspector quiet as to build the shrine.

'From what the sub-inspector said I guessed that the inspector must have drunk the money away in a week. Lal's superior started quoting the law again. "*Muluki Ain*, Part 4, chapter 19, no. 1, six years, three years, one year in jail. The government has fixed the bail money at Rs. 540 per year. Multiply that by six years we'll demand. No one in Dhanee Gaon can pay that!" Well, I was quite puzzled to find the police plotting against the Christian leader, but they'll not find him in Dhanee Gaon by *Dasain* time! I'll make sure he leaves our village well before the festival.'

Renu had listened quietly thus far, but she could not hold her tongue any longer. 'If the police have plotted as you've done, why don't you stop bothering the Christian leader? Let them do the job for you. We've had enough problems already!' Renu shouted again.

'Shh, let's talk of something else . . . Renu, do you feel angry at me because you have to look after the cattle rather than go to school?' Mahila tried to diagnose the cause of her outburst.

'You'd rather drink than buy me books! Of course, I'd like to go to school, I'd like to train as a nurse; but Fate wouldn't have it. They say you can receive only those things written on your forehead or the palms of your hands,' said Renu philosophically.

'Neither your forehead, nor your palms; both look beautiful,' Mahila replied. 'I was afraid your English teacher would make you a Christian. Christians have strange rules. They don't observe our festivals, they don't marry our men or women. They remain aloof. We'd find no husband for you if the whole village turned Christian!'

'Father, marriage hasn't even entered my mind,' Renu lied. 'Besides, when I become a nurse, any idiot will marry me. I

27

have other worries now. I think soon your drinking will land you in jail. What will Mother and I do then?'

'Mother will rejoice to see the drunkard who ill-treats her locked up!' Mahila winked.

'No, she only wishes you to change your ways. She loves you!'

'She loves me? The witch! Why did she eat up your three brothers then? That started me drinking, didn't it?' Mahila snarled.

'Untrue! Mother just has a weak body. Other women in the village have had miscarriages too. Their husbands haven't gone around calling their wives "witches" as you have done.'

'Others haven't eaten up three sons. I could understand losing one or two, but three sons in a row! I've no one to do my funeral rites!' Mahila trembled in anger.

'How come she bore me then?' Renu thought she had made her point.

'Perhaps the witch prefers to eat only boys!' Mahila replied. Renu knew she could not win the argument. She stood up to leave.

'No, you sit down here,' Mahila pleaded. 'Make sure the cattle get fed well. I'll go away. Don't tell your mother what I told you, but ask her to cook something for me. I'll come when darkness sets in! I feel rather hungry.' Mahila stood up, and slung the bag on his shoulder.

'But where shall I say you've gone?' Renu asked, wanting to know more.

'I won't tell you,' Mahila stood up. 'They say women can't keep secrets!' He started walking towards the opening in the raspberry hedge.

'I should've been born a boy,' Renu called after him furiously, 'but Mother would've eaten me up too!' Mahila probably did not hear her angry words. He had disappeared.

Renu walked to the opening of the green plot where the cattle grazed. They did not even look at her. Obviously the grass, more plentiful there than elsewhere, took all their attention.

Renu squinted at the sun. It had now grown too hot for her to sit where her father had been sitting. She went instead to a shady spot next to the pine tree. After she had sat down, she gazed at the hill on the other side of the Trisuli river. Below her lay Dhanee Gaon.

Dhanee Gaon in Trisuli district! Renu lived almost two hours' trek up from the banks of the Trisuli. Trisuli, Trisuli, Trisuli, she thought. The river she worshipped, the town she did her shopping in and the district she lived in all had the same name. She preferred Dhanee Gaon to the Trisuli bazaar. Her village climaxed in a plateau of pine trees. How refreshing to tend cattle and bask in the sun, and watch the eagles circling the deep blue sky!

Meditation on the beauty of her village soon gave way to unpleasant reality. She would never become a nurse nor get to see the hospitals in Kathmandu. Depending on where her husband lived, she would live and die somewhere close to the Trisuli river. As a daughter-in-law, she would go to bed late, get up at four in the morning, fetch water, cook for the entire family, probably do all the washing up, then start the process for the evening meal. The picture of her future drudgery weighed her down. The arguments with her father returned to her mind. Oh, to be a son, she thought, then Father would have someone to perform his funeral rites. Then he'd not torment Mother any more!

Mother had told her of ancient sages who meditated under trees, and received what they wanted. If I meditate enough *Ram* will make me a boy, she thought. She would try it anyway. She sat cross-legged in the shade. She shut her eyes, and concentrated on *Ram*, the god forced to spend fourteen years in the forest because of his step-mother, the god who lost his wife to the demon *Ravan*, the god who divorced his wife because a washer-man accused her of temporarily having *Ravan* as her husband. She could not concentrate. Her mind wandered hopelessly.

She opened her eyes. Another god came to her mind – *Krishna*.

'*Krishna*, make me a boy, make me a boy, make me a boy.' She shut her eyes as she repeated her request. Her thoughts soon went to youthful *Krishna*, stealing yoghurt, flirting with sixteen hundred women. 'Make me a boy, *Krishna*,' she said. She shut her eyes hard, and focused her attention on his flute playing and blue-black body. Renu felt a decade passed while

29

she meditated. She would open her eyes, and find herself a boy. One, two, three!

The calf had come into the plot, and was staring at her. Nothing will ever make me a boy, she thought, as she reached out to the calf. She scratched its neck. The calf, basking in the attention it received, drew even closer.

She had an excuse to take the cattle home early that day. The cattle had found more pasture quickly. Besides, Father had said he would come home for dinner, hadn't he?

Sanumaya sat on a straw mat on the courtyard, and sorted out the spinach she would cook for curry that evening and perhaps the next morning. The late evening sun warmed her back. She looked surprised to see the cattle returning so soon. Renu spoke before Mother could do so.

'Father will come for dinner tonight!'

'Shh! Can you speak more quietly?' Sanumaya scolded her. 'Don't you know we should keep all this a secret?'

'Father will come for dinner, he hasn't run away,' repeated Renu, coming a bit closer.

'He should have gone to my family's home,' Sanumaya suggested. 'He should have taken the police's advice.'

'I got mad with him,' Renu said. 'He said you ate up my three brothers, and that you're a child eater.'

'Did he?' Sanumaya did not show any surprise. 'That's the misery of being a woman. I've heard it so many times from him, it doesn't affect me any more.'

'If I were you, I'd have left him the first time he said such a thing, Mother.'

'If you were me, you'd have continued as I have. You'd have borne all the beating and the bruises. You'd have cried at night, but your eyes would've dried by morning. You'd have fetched water, lit fires, and tried to make your husband as happy as possible.' Mother looked dolefully at her daughter. Renu stared on. 'No sooner does a woman run out with another man than the whole village calls her a prostitute. A man may collect as many spouses as he likes and not suffer for it!'

Mother's quite right, Renu thought, she's quite right.

Sanumaya collected the spinach she had prepared for cooking.

She had not believed Renu's report that her husband would return home for dinner. She had lived with a drunkard too long! However, after dark, Mahila entered his home, and filled his stomach with all the *dhindo* and spinach curry he could get. Renu knew he always found the *dhindo* hard to swallow. His former military life had spoilt him. However, that night he did not complain.

Not having eaten since the night before, it must have tasted good, thought Renu. He must feel very tired and drowsy. However, Father seemed to have hidden strength. After the quick meal, Mahila disappeared into the darkness outside.

'In the end, it's the child eater who has to give him food!' Sanumaya added sarcastically.

CHAPTER THREE

OUT OF HIS MIND

While Renu lay half asleep, her mother was whispering things to her. Frankly, Sanumaya did not know what to make of the change Mahila professed. She thought he had had even more to drink the night before, but admitted that Mahila did not reek of alcohol. Sanumaya had opened the door to him towards midnight. That morning, Mahila lay snoring. The cock had crowed three times already, so Sanumaya had lit her small kerosine lamp and tried to confide in her daughter. Renu was not too responsive, but turned her half-opened eyes towards her father. Even while asleep, he had a fixed smile on his face. This disconcerted Renu somewhat.

Another day had begun. Mother went about her duties. Renu knew her every move. She walked out of the door to the back of her house to urinate. Then she picked up the same water vessel Renu would carry later in the morning, and made her way to the village tap. Pretending to sleep was no use when Mother was away. Renu got up and wondered if Mother would soon use the lion-mouthed stone tap for the last time. When the villagers knew that Father had also turned a Christian, they would surely prohibit the family from using it. In some ways this did not bother her terribly. The Christians had found another spring on the other side of the village. Mother and she could fetch water from there, a destination just a bit further away. However, she dreaded the scorn of the villagers. As she washed her face with a bowl of water over the pit where she cleaned the cooking utensils, Renu could not help uttering a prayer to her Mother's favourite deity.

'Ram, Ram, stop this new madness. One day he beats up the Christian teacher, the next day he joins them!'

Renu heard her mother hum a prayer to *Ram* and enter the

door. This meant she would have to do her turn at the stone tap. The hymn ended when Sanumaya saw Renu up and about.

'Something happened last night when you were asleep, Renu,' whispered Sanumaya. 'I tried to tell you as soon as I woke up, but you were fast asleep.'

'What?' Renu pretended not to know anything.

'Your father says he has now joined the Christians!'

'I don't believe it,' Renu's mouth opened in astonishment. 'Perhaps we'll have more peace now; he won't beat up the Christian leader any more.'

'Less peace, you fool!' Sanumaya retorted. 'The villagers will probably stop us using the tap.'

'He may stop beating you too, Mother,' Renu said. She poured the water Sanumaya had just brought into an earthen vessel nearby, and left for the tap.

The failure of the monsoon the year before had dried up the spring that fed the tap. Her vessel took quite a while to fill up. Renu did not know whether she preferred the present small trickle or the muddy gurgle after the monsoon arrived. She felt fortunate. At her mother's home across the Tarachuli, people walked half an hour just to get one vessel of water. She carried the filled vessel back on her hip. Mother could now milk the cow, start the morning meal, and face the day. Renu felt satisfied after her two trips for water, and started to light a fire.

Renu was clearing the fire-place with iron tongs when Mahila, still rubbing his eyes and yawning, descended.

'You've got up early, Father,' Renu said, trying very hard not to show surprise.

'Yes, I forced myself to get up. I've become a Christian now. Patrus Masih says that I should get up early, read the Bible, and pray. *Yesu* will make me a better person as I do this.' Mahila had a half smile that betrayed his fear that Renu would not trust him. Just then, Sanumaya came with milk scarcely visible at the bottom of the bucket. Mahila had to talk to her somehow.

'I was just telling Renu that I'm a changed man now.'

'This sounds worse than getting drunk! ' Sanumaya burst out. 'You'll not join the group. The villagers will turn against all of us. You may continue to beat me, but don't do anything that will demote you to the lowest of castes, lower than even the Tamangs. The *lamas* will cast a spell on you and make you mad!'

'My *Yesu* can outdo the *lamas*,' Mahila replied.

'What an unfortunate woman I am,' Sanumaya moaned. 'Beatings since fourteen, more beatings after each miscarriage; and as if that wasn't enough, now the villagers will drive us out and make us beggars!'

'Let me explain everything that happened last night,' Mahila said, smiling sheepishly. 'You know the plot of land the Subbhas have donated to the Christians? On it is the straw-roofed, mud and bamboo-plastered church. They couldn't even build it out of stones like our house! After eating last night, I went there. The clouds had eclipsed the moon, and made it dark enough to carry out my plans. I went to the southern wall of the church and stood peering in through a crack. My heart was beating, and I became nervous. All my previous military training hadn't taught me the calm I needed for the task. The northern wall had a wooden cross. A plank of wood below it had painted on it, "I am the Way, the Truth, and the Life". About five feet away on the floor stood a table. On a mat in front of it squatted five men, kneeling on the ground and praying. A kerosine lantern flickered on the table. I didn't expect to find people there. The sight puzzled me.

'Overcome by curiosity, I crept towards the northern side of the hut. I smiled when I saw the fruit of my labour the evening before. Patrus Masih didn't bow his head to the ground as others did. He couldn't. He had two bandages on. One circled his head in an attempt to cover up the wound on his forehead. The other, as a round patch on the cheek below his right ear, almost looked like an ornament. Patrus raised his two hands parallel to his shoulders. A funny way to sit, I thought.

'Out of the semicircle they formed, I heard this fellow Jogbir doing all the talking. Others swayed their heads, and chimed in from time to time with "amen, amen!" I saw Patrus' palms tighten into fists, open up, and close again. I couldn't understand the curious words they mumbled. I had to get closer. I pressed my right ear to the cracks in the plastered wall. Only then could I hear the words.

"Lord, bless Mahila, who has beaten up our pastor. They bruised you more on the cross. By your stripes, we're healed.

Lord, help us to rejoice in our suffering for you."

'What a neat idea! I thought. Since I was still free and not behind bars wasn't I already blessed? Well, I heard all chime the "amen" again, just like a brood of chicks responding to mother hen. Another fellow prayed, "Lord, he's threatened to burn this church down. Deliver us from his plot."

'It was incredible how they seemed to read my mind! I must have said something like that when I was drinking the day before. Another "amen" silenced the second voice which I didn't bother to identify.

'The third voice, low but dignified, belonged to Patrus Masih.

"Lord, bless Mahila. You converted Saul, and made him Paul. You can do the same for Mahila. Lord, paralyse his evil plans against our meeting place. Protect us from arson. Dampen the matches in his pockets!" At this point I wanted to break out into a horse-laugh, but controlled myself. I thought what a silly idiot he was to think I was still old-fashioned enough to use matches. I put my hands into my pocket and felt my cigarette lighter.

'Then I couldn't wait any more. I had to do it before the moon broke through the cloud. I crept back to the southern side of the hut. For a moment I looked at the Himalayan range shining in the distance, then at the Trisuli river which would guide my flight. I intended to walk along its banks, and make my way to Dhading. I'd be a guest of my aunt for a week or two till the matter died down. She'd have no clue as to the arson I had just committed.

'The hot sun had made my job easier. The thatched roof felt crisp, ready to go up in flames at the touch of my cigarette lighter. To take no chances, I had brought along the kerosine bottle hanging on the peg next to the fire-place.' At this point Sanumaya turned her eyes to the peg on the pillar where the bottle had hung. Renu did the same. It had vanished.

'I took the bottle out of my pocket, and felt my heart beating harder. I cursed my stupidity for not having carried out part of my plan when I'd listened to them some time ago. With the bottle in my hand, I crept again parallel to the five deep in prayer.

"Lord, call Mahila to yourself. Make him your disciple...",

I heard someone pleading.

'With my right hand shivering, I poured a little kerosine on the roof at that point. Then I worked my way to the middle and did the same. Finally, back to the base, I emptied the bottle. Out came the cigarette lighter. With my fingers, I made a canopy around it.

"One. . . two. . . three," I whispered as I struck. A spark escaped from the lighter; however, it didn't ignite the petrol-soaked wick. My lighter had the habit of lighting up on the second or third try. Another spark! My fault that time – in my excitement the canopy of nine fingers hadn't held. I struck again. No spark. Again, and again, and again! In despair, I beat my forehead with the palm of my hand. The nine cigarettes I'd consumed during the day had used up all the flint!

'Resisting the temptation to hurl the lighter into the maize field, I put it back into my pocket. It had never before failed me. I blamed my stupidity. I should have checked the flint while I was at home. I had spare ones there! I thought I'd have to accomplish the project another day. Shame enveloped me. I couldn't even set a hut on fire!

'My plans had misfired. I crept back within earshot of the five who were praying. I smelled the kerosine I had just poured out. What I heard next riveted me.

"Lord, protect us! The communists wanted to burn down the church in Bartandi. You preserved them. To protect your people, you allowed a truck to run over their leader." My heart began to beat faster. A strange fear gripped me. Someone then prayed, "Lord, let nothing evil befall Mahila. Remove the hatred from his heart. Save him!"

'A cold chill went down my spine. A truck ran over the communist leader, and I'm still alive! I thought. I peeped in through the crack in the plaster. I felt something like a magnet at the centre of those praying. Like a steel pin, I wanted to rush to it. I wanted to go in, and tell all! I felt subdued by a power I didn't understand. Patrus Masih may have his revenge, others in the village may laugh, but I must go in! I thought. Within seconds I felt myself running to the door on the other side. To the utter consternation of the five praying, I rushed in and rolled on the floor weeping.

''Thank you Yesu,'' exclaimed someone, as much in fear and confusion as in prayer. Flat on my stomach, I covered my face and sobbed bitterly.'

'Should that make you a Christian?' Sanumaya looked with pleading eyes.

'I haven't finished,' Mahila said. 'I kept on wailing and weeping like a baby. For a few minutes I didn't know what to do, but Patrus Masih told me how to wash my sins away by trusting in *Yesu*. I repeated after him, ''*Yesu*, take my sins away, take my life.'' I believe *Yesu* changed me that same minute. Such joy and peace now!'

'Peace!' screamed Sanumaya. 'Wait till the villagers spit at us and forbid us to use the water tap.'

'What does it matter?' Mahila sounded indifferent.

'Water in the morning, will you go to fetch it?'

'Yes,' replied Mahila.

'Yes, you will! After we've brought a bowl of it to your bed to wash your face.' Sanumaya ground her teeth.

Puzzled, Renu poured out the tea. She did not know which side to take in this parental dispute. Sanumaya picked up the tea cup, and put it on the floor again. Mahila drank, and got up, looking just as confused.

'I'm going to meet Patrus Masih. I want to ask a lot of questions, learn a lot. In two months' time, I'll wash myself in the river. That'll make me a real Christian. Renu, I'll come for my rice at about ten o'clock.' Mahila's figure disappeared into the orange sunlight that had just made the Tarachuli summit glow.

Like most other Nepali women, Mother appeared docile most of the time; but like them, she knew when to act. She felt her world was falling apart. She had to do something. She finished her tea in four gulps, and rushed upstairs. A few seconds later Renu saw Mother running down.

'Renu, you cook this morning. I'm going out.'

'Where?' asked Renu in surprise.

'None of your business; do as I tell you!' retorted Sanumaya. Renu felt her father's temper had now entered her mother. She saw Mother wrap the light shawl around her. The *Falgun* sun did make it unnecessary. The shawl only gave Mother a more dignified look.

* * *

Renu sighed with relief when Mother returned so quickly.
She did not enjoy cooking. She would rather fetch water a
hundred times. When Mother took over, there was only the
rice to be cooked. However, Renu still could not gauge the
right amount of water to boil the rice in, and so gladly left the
most difficult job for Sanumaya. Instead, she carried the water
vessel again on her left hip as she had done a thousand times
before, and bounced off to water the cattle.

When Renu returned with water, she saw Father seated and
mumbling on the verandah. He held a black book in his left
hand, and read it like a wizard. Renu caught only the first line
she heard, 'For God so loved the world that He gave His only
Son...' Father was too fast for her. She wondered who this God
was.

Renu did not want to appear nosy. She walked past Father
on the courtyard to the place where the cattle stood tied. After
filling the water trough, she rushed in to help Mother get the
kitchen ready. She put the low wooden stools in their places.
Sanumaya dished out the food on the brass saucer-like plates.
A smell Renu did not expect came to her nose.

Mother had avenged herself on Father by cooking *dhindo!*
He had eaten it reluctantly the night before. Renu expected
Father to flare up any moment. Mahila looked indifferent.
Instead, he put his right hand to the *dhindo*, made a ball, dipped
it into the spinach soup, and threw it into his mouth. Renu
watched with her hand fixed to her plate. Mahila repeated the
process. Again, and again, and again!

A tear rolled down Renu's right cheek and into her food.
She turned her face so that her parents did not see it. She cursed
herself for not cooking faster, for not having finished the rice
before Mother returned. Renu resolved to do the cooking,
however poor, in the evening.

Father's hands had not dried when the *Pradhan Panch*, his
distant uncle, arrived. He wiped his palms on the sides of his
shirt, and joined them in a greeting.

'*Namasthe!*'

'*Namasthe!*' The *Pradhan Panch* returned the greeting. Mahila asked Renu to bring out the cotton cushion. When Renu brought it, Mahila offered it to the *Pradhan Panch*, but he himself sat on the straw mat. The *Pradhan Panch* looked old enough to have fathered Mahila. He coughed frequently, more to radiate a gentlemanly air than to relieve his chest.

The *Pradhan Panch* talked in a soft voice. Renu made frequent trips back and forth: kitchen, verandah, courtyard, verandah, kitchen. She did not catch any of the conversation. She gave up, and squatted in the corner of the courtyard, in front of the pit where she did the washing. Out of the corner of her eye, she could see the *Pradhan Panch* remonstrating with both his hands. Now and then the *Pradhan Panch* shook his finger at Mahila in warning. At one point Mahila quickly flipped through the pages of his black book. He did not find what he wanted, and put it down.

As Father grew more stubborn, the *Pradhan Panch* raised his voice. Renu pricked up her ears.

'What glory Nepal has as the only Hindu kingdom in the world! You've turned a traitor!' The *Pradhan Panch* could not have been more blunt.

'That doesn't mean only Hindus live in Nepal,' Mahila replied. 'We have Muslims and Christians too.'

'Let the police understand that! They can lock you up for at least a year.' The *Pradhan Panch* again pointed his finger at Mahila.

'At the end of the day, whether a deity can help you or not matters,' Mahila put forward his case. 'The Hindu gods couldn't stop me from drinking and beating up my wife. *Yesu* changed me!'

'Many have stopped beating their wives without forsaking the religion of their ancestors,' the *Pradhan Panch* replied. 'You've only followed *Yesu* for one day. You wait and see.'

Renu realised the *Pradhan Panch* was not getting anywhere. She feared for her father. The *Pradhan Panch* ruled like the king of the village. Not obeying him could spell disaster.

The *Pradhan Panch* lowered his voice a bit as if to indicate he had embarrassed Mahila enough. Mahila listened, answered in one or two words. Mostly he nodded.

From the seclusion of the kitchen, Mother decided she had heard enough of the ill-fated conversation.

'It's midday already, Renu, take the cattle out,' she called to her daughter.

'I haven't finished the pots and pans yet.' Renu shouted to make herself audible. Sanumaya came out of the door, bowed a *namasthe* to the *Pradhan Panch*, and dashed to Renu's side. Renu realised that Mother did not intend to do the washing up. She merely wanted to make her presence felt.

The *Pradhan Panch* had talked enough. 'I've said what I should for your own good, Mahila! We don't want to see you end up in jail.'

'Neither do I, but I'll not desert *Yesu*,' Mahila replied rather sheepishly.

'You're out of your mind. Our gods have made you mad for deserting them. Keep it up,' the *Pradhan Panch* remarked sarcastically as he stood up. Mahila kept quiet. Sanumaya made another *namasthe* to the *Pradhan Panch*, as he left. Renu despised and admired her father for his stubbornness. What attracted him to this *Yesu*? Renu wanted to know.

CHAPTER
FOUR

GREAT CHANGE

Mother was crying. Renu knew she had caused it. Two months had passed. The Saturday before, Renu had accompanied her father to the church. Sanumaya allowed her to go. She thought Renu's curiosity would wane after her daughter saw the place where her father made a fool of himself every week. That Saturday Renu wanted to go again!

Renu quickly finished the washing up which was her duty each day after a meal. She brought in the pots and pans, and put them neatly on the wooden shelf blackened by the soot of the fire. Mother wiped her running nose. Renu wanted to hurry upstairs and dress up.

'Out of all my children, only you have survived. Will you pierce my heart too?' Sanumaya turned her wet eyes at her daughter.

'I don't want to pierce anybody's heart,' Renu shrugged. 'I just want to know more about what Father believes. How can I find out whether he's done the right thing or not unless I know his religion fully?'

'What miserable luck!' Sanumaya moaned. 'I asked the *Pradhan Panch* to intervene. I spent sixty rupees on the lama, even bought a rooster for sacrifice. Nothing stopped your father's madness. Now you want to go to the church too!'

'You asked me to go to the tap the Christians use, didn't you?' Renu reminded her mother.

'Yes, the villagers knew about your father's conversion the first Saturday he went to church. They started saying the water supply would dry up if we used their tap. I had no choice,' replied Sanumaya.

'Well, I wouldn't have seen Patrus Masih's daughter Sushila if you hadn't sent me there. We met each other every day at school till Father took me out. She invited me to Sunday school last Saturday. I didn't find anything evil there as you suggested. Shouldn't I go if a school friend invites me?' Renu looked at her mother then at the ladder she wanted to climb to change her clothes.

'Did she invite you again this week?' Sanumaya asked.

'Yes, she wants me to help her keep the children in order. Sushila helped me a lot at school. Shouldn't I do at least that in return?'

'But she wants to make you a Christian?' Sanumaya got to the point.

'No one can make me one by force,' Renu replied. 'I'm fifteen now, and can think for myself at least a little bit. Besides, Father has stopped smoking, getting drunk, and beating you. You can now go to bed each day without sore limbs. What do you find wrong with Christians?'

'I'd rather endure blows than see your father in the church.' Sanumaya stared into the sunlight out of the door.

'You've forgotten the beatings so quickly.' Renu put a foot on the ladder. Sanumaya kept quiet. Plastering the space around the fire-place with the mixture of red clay and cow dung had taken longer than usual. It remained unfinished when Renu came down dressed.

Renu noticed Mother gazing at the shoulder bag she had taken to school until the previous year. Now it carried her New Testament.

'While Patrus Masih teaches in the church, we go to Sunday school. We sing, Sudeep tells a story, I just try to keep the children listening and quiet!' Renu assured Sanumaya.

'Who's this Sudeep?' asked Sanumaya, finishing her plastering of the area around the fire-place. She washed her hands in the pot that had the wet rag and the mixture.

'Sushila's younger brother,' replied Renu. 'Last Saturday he told the story of the small train in Darjeeling. It starts from a town called Siliguri, right in the plains. It winds upwards in countless loops. It keeps on moving as long as the driver keeps feeding it with coal. Sudeep said that Yesu gives us the same power as the coal to the train . . . Father must have reached the church a long time ago. I must go!'

Renu would take some time to get used to the Nepali

Christian culture she encountered within the four walls of the church. To the *Jai Masih* greeting from the two ushers at the door of the church, she responded with her *namasthe*. She followed Sushila who led her to the front, left-hand side of the hut. Other women folk had already gathered. The lucky ones avoided backache by choosing seats that allowed leaning against the wall. Such places in the front were already full. Cross-legged, Renu sat down on the straw mat. She saw her father with other men on the right-hand side. He was quietly murmuring a portion from the New Testament, and swaying his head up and down to read even faster. Having experienced the service the previous Saturday, Renu knew more or less what to expect.

The service began when Patrus Masih entered, and stood in front of the table. The low murmur of the congregation died down. Patrus turned to the back of the New Testament, read the six verses from Psalm 23. Then the service took its course: hymn number 1, the welcome, notices with the plea for all to attend the house fellowship on Wednesday evenings, hymn number 32, reading from the Bible, the offertory hymn, a time of prayer, hymn number 17 during which the children left for Sunday school. Patrus Masih rose to preach.

Sushila and Sudeep held Sunday school on the verandah of Karna Tamang's home. Roughly a dozen young boys and girls of all ages followed Sushila towards the mat which Thuli, Karna's wife, had set. Thuli herself did not go to church, but did not object to Karna's piety. Her son Mangal and daughter Sabita sat with the other Sunday school children. She remained content with what she heard right at her door step.

Sudeep finally arrived carrying a black box the shape of an elongated pumpkin, like those which grew on top of the roof above the verandah. He ceremoniously placed the box on the ground, and revealed the musical instrument inside. 'We'll sing,' he said. 'My friend brought this from Darjeeling two days ago. We have lots of these there. It has six metal strings. What shall we sing?'

'Great change since I was born!' suggested one. Sudeep began, and the rest joined in, 'Great change/ since I was born . . . things I used to do/ I do them no more . . . places I used to go/ I go there no more . . .' After sometime, Sudeep raised his

45

right hand to stop the group singing further. 'I don't like some words in this song. Somebody translated this from English. Following *Yesu* doesn't mean you stop doing everything and live in a vacuum. Rather, following *Yesu* implies doing certain things as well. After "Great change/ since I was born," we will sing, "I did not pray/ I pray to *Yesu* now . . . I did not love/ I love others now . . ."' Sudeep evidently excelled in spontaneous compositions.

Renu did not like the improvisations, but she sang them anyway. She had not seen the guitar before, but felt the group sang better with it. After a bit of fumbling, Shankar made the *madal* fit the song. Renu marvelled at Sudeep's musical talent. She knew the *madal* too well to admire its player.

When the chorus ended, Shankar blurted out, 'Sudeep *dai* should sing a song by himself!' Sudeep hesitated or appeared to do so. He forced a gentlemanly cough, and could not resist introducing his song.

'The Christian life demands everything. We have to endure much hardship, suffering, persecution. About two months ago my father received blows from a drunkard . . .' Renu saw Sushila cross her right forefinger on her lips, and make gestures to Sudeep. Quite oblivious to her warning, he continued, 'But when we go to heaven, *Yesu* will wipe our tears away . . . . . .' Sudeep started strumming his instrument. Then broke out his melodious voice. The song described heaven. Renu thought she saw it.

'No more tears in heaven/ no more anxiety,' Sudeep sang, 'only people washed/ in the Blood remain there.'

I left Mother crying at home, Renu thought. She should have come to listen to this!

After the clapping in honour of Sudeep had subsided, Sushila began her story. She told of a young boy who brought his lunch to *Yesu*. *Yesu* took it, and fed five thousand people with it. Renu felt too distracted to be amazed by the miracle. Darjeeling must resemble heaven if people there can sing like this, she thought.

Sushila ended the story with a moral lesson – give all you have to *Yesu*, and He'll multiply it much much more.

When the last song ended and the children dispersed, Renu saw Sushila take Sudeep aside. Sushila whispered something to him for a while. 'I'll do as you say,' Renu barely heard Sudeep answer. The next moment, both Sushila and Sudeep walked towards her. Sushila broke the silence.

'Sudeep has to ask your forgiveness for what he said about your father.' Before Renu could respond, Sudeep blurted out, *'Bahini*, please forgive me. I didn't know Mahila was your father. You came last Saturday, but I didn't ask about your family. We rejoice that your father comes to church now.'

'What you said didn't do me any harm,' Renu said with a blush, not knowing how to respond to the first apology she had ever received. 'My father did many nasty things when he was drunk!' Just then, the church service ended.

Renu saw her father talk to a man she thought she had seen before, recognising him by the type of green canvas boots he had on.

'Come again, next Saturday,' Renu heard her father say. The man nodded a yes, and departed with a *namasthe*. Renu, still puzzled that Sudeep had apologised to her for seemingly such a small thing, walked to her father. 'Who's that man?' Renu asked.

'A policeman in plain clothes,' Mahila replied.

'How do you know?' Renu sounded incredulous.

'He came with the other officer to arrest me some months ago. I had to part with quite a sum of money that day. The same fellow . . . Renu, go home and help Mother. I have to go to my baptism class. Also, I'd better tell the pastor about this man.'

CHAPTER
FIVE

BURNING THE BRIDGES

Renu knew Patrus Masih wanted to make her father's baptism a festive occasion. She did not know the full significance of the ceremony, but shared in her father's enthusiasm. Often in his preaching, Patrus had compared the ex-sergeant's conversion with that of the central figure in the Acts of the Apostles, a book in the Bible. In Mahila, Patrus found a vivid example of a persecutor turned preserver, a Saul into Paul. Father had shown a lot of interest in the baptismal classes held every Tuesday for the previous two months. The time for him to take the dip, as witness of his loyalty to *Yesu*, approached.

Instinctively, Patrus had chosen the first month, *Baisakh*, of the Nepali new year for Father's baptism and spiritual meetings. The relatively light farm work during that month inspired Patrus to settle for this although the four-year-old church at Dhanee Gaon had not conducted special meetings previously. Renu had heard that churches all over Nepal held them when the Hindus had their own celebrations. The government gave holidays for Hindu festivals but not Christian ones.

Rather than baptise her father himself, Patrus decided to give the honour to a pastor from Kathmandu. Pastor Gangaram, the guest, would begin by baptising Mahila on the Sunday morning after his arrival. That very evening the special meetings would begin. The holy communion service the following Saturday would bring the meetings to a close. Her father had confided secrets to her which only a few leaders of the congregation knew.

Father had also told Renu the various illustrations Patrus had used during the last baptismal class to drive home the meaning of the ceremony he would soon undergo.

'If I cross the bridge and set fire to the wooden posts, what will happen?' Patrus had asked.

'The bridge will burn and fall into the river,' Mahila had replied.

'Can I come back to this side of the bridge again?'

'No,' Mahila had answered.

'Baptism has the same effect. It destroys the bridge to the past life,' Patrus had continued. 'The dip in the river symbolises your death. Your emerging from the water indicates the new life you've received by the power of *Yesu*.' Renu could not visualise the second illustration too well. The pastor had compared the Christian to a cyclist. 'As soon as the cyclist stops pedalling, he falls down!' he had told Mahila. Renu imagined the urchins cycling on the cobbled streets of Trisuli. Patrus wanted her father to keep on progressing in the new life he had adopted.

The service that Saturday was the object of much anticipation. Patrus gave the notices: the guest pastor would arrive that evening, the special meetings would start the next night, anyone willing to provide hospitality to the three believers beyond the Tarachuli should meet the pastor's wife after the service, all should pray for the coming 'Jordan experience' of a certain member. Renu saw Father smile at hearing the last announcement. Then for some reason he looked a bit worried.

After the offertory hymn, Renu followed the children out to their Sunday school. Sudeep, carrying the guitar which greatly attracted the children, headed the group. Shankar followed. Hurrying, Renu caught up with Sudeep walking to the verandah of Thuli's home.

'Please sing your song of heaven, *dai*,' asked Renu, overcoming her shyness.

'Not every Saturday,' replied Sudeep. He looked back and saw Sushila, his sister, approaching. 'We should meet and talk sometime,' he added hastily in a muted voice. Renu blushed. Sudeep tuned a stray string on the guitar, and began chorus singing.

The Sunday school finished later than the service that day. Renu saw her father waiting for her. When she arrived, both started their walk back home.

'Father, you looked worried just before I left for Sunday

school,' Renu noted. 'What was the matter?'

'I saw a man with short hair sitting a few rows behind me. He looked quite unfamiliar. He could be a policeman in disguise,' answered Mahila.

'Well, the church is for policemen as well, isn't it? I'm not worried. I realised that the pastor was referring to your baptism when he mentioned a "certain member". Why did he say "the Jordan experience"?' Renu asked.

'Perhaps to keep the baptism a secret from the police,' Mahila replied. 'The ceremony consists of a person going into the water and coming out again, similar to our Lord's baptism in the Jordan river. Patrus taught me that the dip symbolises death and burial of the old self, the sinful person. Coming out of the water stands for having new life through *Yesu*.'

'Oh yes. You've told me those things from your baptismal classes. Have all Christians taken part in this ceremony?'

'Not all, only those who take the Lord's supper,' Mahila replied. He hesitated, then went on.

'Well, the pastor told me to tell no one, but I can't keep secrets from you. You can pray for me,' he continued. 'I can now confirm that I'm to be baptised tomorrow morning by this pastor from Kathmandu. Don't let your mother know. She'll have a fit. She hates me. She would rather have me drunk than follow *Yesu*.'

'That'll make you a "full" Christian, will it? Then you can take part in the Lord's supper too!' Renu seemed as delighted as her father was concerned.

Mother had timed it perfectly. When Mahila and Renu arrived on the courtyard of their home, they saw Sanumaya, carrying the brass vessel on her hip and walking away to the tap. When they were together, she talked only about essentials with Renu. Her conversations with Mahila mostly ended in arguments. Sanumaya tried to avoid them both when possible.

Renu saw Father go to the cattle stall and loosen the animals.

'Keep a watch on the house, Renu,' Mahila said, as he led the cow and the buffalo away. He chose to leave the calf tied on the peg in the courtyard.

Renu decided to make use of this rare moment of leisure to

pray. She went up the ladder, sat on her bed, and turned in her New Testament to Matthew 7. Sushila had said something about two houses – one built on sand, one built on rock. Both seemed ludicrous to Renu. To illustrate, Sushila had drawn two pictures. One had a house just ten feet away from the water on the shore of the Trisuli river. The other portrayed a house on the summit of Tarachuli. Renu had to read quite a bit to get to the section she liked: 'Therefore everyone who hears these words of mine and acts upon them, may be compared to a wise man who built his house upon a rock . . .'

She imagined herself living in a house on top of the Tarachuli summit. The monsoon came in torrents. The Trisuli river flooded and rose up. It washed away paddy fields and houses close to its banks, then the entire village of Dhanee Gaon. The wind whistled. Lightning flashed. Nothing touched her house. Renu remained safe . . . with Sudeep! Oh, the thought of him! said Renu to herself, I want to pray for Father.

Renu pulled the pillow out of her bed, and with it cushioned her back against the wall. As taught to pray in Sunday school, she shut her eyes and whispered, 'Lord God, bless Father tomorrow morning. Make the baptism a great event for him. Let him die with *Yesu* and rise with Him. Bless our pastor who will take him to the water . . .'

Renu jerked herself and opened her eyes. What a foolish girl! she scolded herself, I almost fell asleep while praying. She decided to pray aloud. 'Lord *Yesu*, protect my father tomorrow morning. Keep away people who shouldn't see the baptism. Bless Father. May he follow you even more closely . . .'

She started, and felt scared all of a sudden. The ladder creaked. Resting her right hand on the top rung, Sanumaya appeared. 'So, a second Christian in the house! You too have followed your father's footsteps, you rebellious witch!'

Renu sat nonplussed. Mother had seen her go to church for eight Saturdays already. Renu did not understand the cause of the outburst.

'I . . . I was praying, Mother,' Renu stuttered.

'Yes, of course!' growled Sanumaya.

Renu saw her mother with cheeks red, her right hand stretched out, rushing to her. Everything else happened too quickly. The next moment Renu felt her forehead touch the uncovered planks of her cot. Sanumaya clenched Renu's lock of hair firmly in her right palm. Once, twice, three times! Sanumaya banged her daughter's forehead on the planks. Her anger had not yet dissipated. Still pulling Renu by the hair, Sanumaya began dragging her off the bed to the mud floor. Renu smelled the red clay and the cow dung mixture as her knees fell to the floor with a thud. Sanumaya let go of the lock of hair, and stamped on Renu's head with the sole of her dusty right foot. Renu's hair turned brown.

'Continue praying for that drunkard.' Sanumaya gritted her teeth. 'I'd rather kill you than see you disgrace me!'

After crawling on all fours for a few seconds, Renu sat with her legs stretched out. She turned towards her bed. Next to the pillow lay her black New Testament. Sanumaya's eyes followed hers more rapidly. Charging like a buffalo irritated by a horse, Sanumaya snatched up the book. She flicked open the hard cardboard cover. With her right hand, she ripped off the pages, nervously clutching at about a dozen pages at a time.

'There, there, there!' Sanumaya snarled. Impatient with the progress, she caught the remaining pages with the hard covers flapping against each other, and in a flash, hurled them through the window. Renu heard the pages flutter in the air and neighbours' chickens down below rush clucking to safety.

Uttering curses, Sanumaya walked to her wooden chest. With the key on a piece of string around her neck, she opened the chest and took her shawl out. Puzzled and too shocked to cry, Renu watched her mother for a few seconds. Then she wiped her swollen forehead with the tip of her *fariah*.

'Let's see how he'll make himself a Christian!' Sanumaya threatened and stamped again on the rungs of the ladder. As she descended, Renu dashed to the window. Her mother seemed to vanish as quickly as she had materialized.

***

While Renu waited, Mahila knocked. Esther, Patrus' wife, had taught him to do so instead of hollering, 'Who is inside?' The bolt clicked, and the door opened. Through the haze of kerosine smoke, Mahila and Renu saw Sudeep peering at

53

them. 'Mahila *dai* and Renu have come,' Sudeep announced and took his place at the table.

'Oh, Mahila!' Patrus exclaimed. 'Esther, bring that chair for him.' Renu walked over to Esther and Sushila. Mahila sat uneasily on the chair.

'I have come a bit late to you, Pastor *dai*.' Mahila struggled. 'When . . . when I returned from grazing the cattle this afternoon, I found Renu crying on her bed. Her forehead's swollen.'

'Of course,' said Esther, gazing intently at Renu. 'I was wondering why she looked so sad. What happened?'

'Her mother beat her. Sanumaya had never done such a thing before. The poor girl did not know how to defend herself.' Both Esther and Sushila began inspecting Renu's forehead.

'How terrible!' Esther consoled him. 'Fortunately, there's no cut in the skin. The devil has done all he can to discourage you, Mahila.'

'Yes, *didi*,' Mahila moaned. Renu thought her father would break into a sob, but the ex-soldier controlled himself. She had quietly begun to weep.

'I'd have starved if Renu hadn't cooked. Only she's left to love me! I wonder what'll happen when my daughter marries and goes to somebody else's home,' Mahila speculated mournfully. Renu began to weep even more.

'Oh, we all love you,' corrected Patrus. 'You're part of this bigger family in *Yesu*.'

'Of course. I was just thinking of my own family,' Mahila continued. 'My wife's done all she could to get me back into Hinduism. She's spent a lot on the *lamas*. I find charmed flower petals and rice grains on my head most mornings.'

After she had wiped away her tears, Renu noticed that the arrival of the guest speaker had caused as much flurry in Esther's home as does the visit of a general to a remote military outpost. The person seated opposite Patrus at the table surprised her by his youthful, energetic looks.

Father had related to her how he had taken some time to get used to the new culture he met in Patrus' home. Now she experienced it. They still ate using the fingers of the right hand, but they had given up squatting or sitting cross-legged on a low wooden stool. The west had met the east, and settled for a compromise.

All were busy. Fifteen fingers dipped vigorously into the plates on the table. No one could persuade Esther to eat with the guest and the people she and Sushila served. Renu kept herself occupied at the sink. Dhanee Gaon did not have piped water. Renu poured water onto the utensils she washed with a small worn-out mug. Those eating made a strange rhythm cutting away at the rice hill on the plates, mixing it in the chicken gravy, shoving each handful into the mouth, sucking the marrow from the chicken bones, and licking the busy fingers.

Renu felt Patrus had to say something to ease Mahila's nervousness.

'Gangaram*ji*, he caused this,' said Patrus, pointing to the scar on his forehead. 'Since then, I've given up teaching at school. Esther wouldn't allow me to go a yard away from home. However, now he has become a child of God. As such, he's our dear brother. You'll baptise him tomorrow.' Renu saw her father cringe a bit.

'Glory to God,' Gangaram added, 'Mahila *bhai*, will you take a new name?'

'No,' interrupted Patrus with a twinkle in his eyes. 'Even you've not changed your name, why should he? Mahila, do you know what *Gangaram* means?'

'Yes,' nodded Mahila. '*Ganga*, the holy river of the Hindus, flows through India. I bathed in it during the war. *Ram*, the name of the Hindu god my wife worships!'

'So he's as Hindu as a *Brahmin*,' added Patrus. 'He just adds the title "Pastor" to become a Christian!' Sudeep led the modest laughter that followed.

'Anyway, you won't take a new name, will you?' Gangaram asked just to make sure.

'No,' Patrus answered again for Mahila. 'Receiving a new heart matters more. *Hallelujah!*'

'Has anyone else in your home believed in the Lord *Yesu*, Mahila *bhai*?' Gangaram looked at Mahila with inquisitive eyes. Renu knew she would be the next topic of conversation. Gangaram had finished eating, but was still licking the fingers of his right hand. Patrus and Sudeep had finished too, but waited.

'No . . . in fact, my daughter comes regularly to Sunday school; but she hasn't made a decision yet.' Mahila seemed torn inside.

'She plays an active role with the children. Let's pray and see. Who knows if she may not soon follow her father to the Jordan,' Patrus expressed more of his hope than reality. Renu blushed and pretended not to hear.

'We have to bind the devil for tomorrow, haven't we, *Rajah*,' Esther suggested.

'Certainly. Let's pray for security and God's blessing for tomorrow . . . Mahila, have you eaten? I forgot to ask till now.' Patrus looked ashamed.

'I haven't, but I'd rather go home, and help Renu put together a meal. Sanumaya went somewhere after beating her daughter. I came here with Renu because I had to know the plans for tomorrow and pray with pastor *dai* from Kathmandu. Also, I couldn't leave Renu alone in the present circumstances.'

Esther, Sushila, and Renu started clearing the table. Renu would not eat anything. Esther was sensitive enough not to force her. She put a little chicken curry in a bowl. 'Take this and share it with your mother,' Esther said solemnly. 'Perhaps this'll cheer her up.' Renu put on a faint smile, but did not answer.

Renu noticed that the men's hands had dried after the meal. They still chatted as if they were seeing each other for the last time. At last Patrus led Gangaram outside the house, across the courtyard. Sushila followed quickly and poured water over their hands on the other side of the stone fence into the maize field. Gangaram picked up the towel from her shoulder. 'It seems more convenient to pray on the verandah,' Gangaram suggested. Mahila ran in to bring the straw mat.

Esther and Sushila had to eat, and so did not join in the praying. With some gentle persuasion, Esther had succeeded in getting Renu to taste a little bit of her renowned cooking. Through the main door, Renu saw Sudeep, Gangaram, Mahila, and Patrus kneel on the mat. To her surprise Patrus began by praying for her. He begged God to change Sanumaya's heart and asked for security and protection during the baptism service the next day. He bound the devil in the name of *Yesu*.

Renu could not really enjoy the food she ate. Now and then she stared into the space beyond the door. She thought she noticed a man's head peep over the stone fence. She rubbed her eyes, wondering if they had deceived her.

Earlier than usual and right at the second cock-crow the next morning, Renu heard Father get up. Mother stirred a bit, but still lay sound asleep. Renu heard him descend the ladder, but remained in bed. She had an excuse – her swollen forehead ached at every movement of her head. She knew where Father was going. She tried to imagine how the Trisuli river would compare with the Jordan. She decided Trisuli would be cleaner and cooler. Right from her bed, she prayed, 'Lord *Yesu*, protect my father from harm; Lord *Yesu*, protect . . . Father . . . Jordan . . .' Soon she dozed off.

CHAPTER
SIX

REMORSE

Renu balanced the water vessel on her left hip, and started the journey home. She did not usually come to the tap during that part of the day, but the cattle looked thirsty. Mother's rough treatment of her the previous day gave her no desire to lead the animals to the pastures. Her swollen forehead made her look sullen as well. During the morning meal, she had just answered her mother as briefly as she could, and then gone about her duties.

The family had begun to use the water tap the Christians used. It brought her quite close to the church. She dreaded meeting Sushila that day lest she should ask again about her forehead. As a precaution, she took a longer path that wound away from the church. This way she hoped she might even get a glimpse of her father and the pastors who had gone for the baptism that morning. She could not understand the delay.

How she wished she had a watch! Already, the sun had begun to descend. She made it about two o'clock. She gazed at the path that led downhill to the Trisuli river, right up to the bazaar. After a while, she saw a familiar face. Renu deliberately reduced her pace to meet him at the crossing. She loosened her grip on the water vessel.

'Namasthe, Karna dai', Renu greeted the man as he approached her. 'Has the Jordan experience ended?' Panting from his climb, Karna did not answer. Instead, he stared at her dolefully.

'My father and the pastors couldn't catch up with you, I bet,' Renu added.

'What shall I say, what shall I say?' Karna asked himself mournfully. 'A disaster! I wish you didn't have to hear about it.' Karna's pale face indicated the seriousness of the matter.

'What? Karna *dai*, please don't keep me in suspense, tell me what's the matter.'

'The police arrested all of us!' Karna replied.

'How come you are here? Do you have to return?'

'No,' Karna started to sob, 'I've denied the Lord!' Renu did not know what to do when a man over twice as old as she wept. She wriggled her body in discomfort. Some water spilled over from the vessel to her clothes.

'Where have they taken Father and the pastors?' Renu asked after a while.

'They were sitting under the banyan tree in the barracks compound when I left them,' Karna replied, taking control of himself. 'I have to go and give news to Esther *didi*. We have to take clothes and bedding to them. I'll come to your home later.' Like a dog just bitten by a bitch, Karna turned left at the crossing towards the church.

Renu had to break the news to Mother. How she wanted to forget the event of the day before, and restore a normal relationship!

'A thousand times I told my idiot of a husband not to follow the foreign religion,' Sanumaya blew up in a rage when she heard of the arrest. 'He avoided all work at home and ran to the church day and night. Now, let him enjoy the free rations the police give him!'

'Mother, Karna *dai* said he would come to our home to take some bedding for Father. Let's go up and pack up some.'

'You do it,' Sanumaya replied. 'I've never packed up bedding before. Neither have I ventured beyond my native place or the Trisuli bazaar!'

Renu climbed up the creaking ladder drowning Mother's mumble down below, and decided to have a try.

'*Nani*,' Renu heard a feeble voice call. She looked out of the window. Esther, Karna, Sudeep! Why Sudeep? Renu ran down the ladder. Sanumaya had already met the group at the verandah, and spread out the straw mat. Esther sat down, and beckoned Karna and Sudeep to do the same.

'A terrible tragedy!' Esther began. 'I think Karna told Renu about it. Did he?' Sanumaya nodded her head in silence.

'Well, we have to do something fast before the sun goes down on us. We should send the men their bedding and things

60

like towels and soap. Karna can take them down.'

'Not I,' replied Karna covering his face. 'I've betrayed my Lord! I can't face the pastors any more.'

'Oh, come Karna,' Esther replied. 'Didn't you pray to *Yesu* and ask for His forgiveness?'

'I did.'

'Hasn't He forgiven you?'

'He has,' Karna replied through his tears.

'Well, then forget about it,' Esther looked at him consolingly. 'Let's do something to help the men.'

'What will the other Christians say?' Karna continued sobbing. 'I've betrayed the Lord!'

'The Bible says that we should leave the past behind and press on to the future. Oh, stop it.' Esther sounded irritated.

'When I left the police barracks, I felt I was the vilest coward in the world. I walked along the river; and, hoping that the pastors, Mahila, and Jogbir would come, waited in a shady spot on its bank. Obviously, they didn't deny the Lord as I did. The police didn't release them.'

'Well, the Lord has forgiven you. You should praise Him for that,' Esther tried again to get on with the business.

'I intended just to say that I'd observe the religion of my forefathers, and continue as a Christian. However, the police asked me things I didn't imagine. I ended up saying that I'd no longer worship *Yesu!*' Karna put his hands to his face again, and moaned loudly.

'Patrus of the Bible denied our Lord, too. You did it once. He did it three times. Won't He restore you as He did Patrus?' Sudeep took his turn at consolation.

'He will,' replied Karna in a soft voice. Sudeep had struck the right chord.

'Have you collected some bedding for your father?' Esther asked Renu, trying to take control of the situation.

'I have, I'll bring it down.'

As Renu walked up the ladder, she heard Karna sob again.

Renu put soap and a towel in Mother's shoulder bag, and tied up the bedding. Within a few minutes, she appeared in front of Karna whose eyes, now dry, showed disapproval of the bundle. 'We'll have to tie it again,' Karna said, looking at Sudeep. 'We can put the soap and towel in it too. Let's make it smaller and neater.'

Meanwhile, Esther was comforting Sanumaya. 'Strange things happen, but our Lord still controls the universe,' Esther said. 'I rejoice that He considered my husband also worthy of arrest. Just baptised, Mahila is like a newly born baby. My husband and Pastor Gangaram can comfort him. Jogbir can cheer him up!'

'You Christians say funny things indeed,' Sanumaya said in a patronising voice. 'Here, the police have taken your husband, yet you say you rejoice!'

'I'd rather the arrest hadn't taken place at all. But as it has, I thank God that Mahila didn't have to face it alone. Will it help matters if I walk about with a sooty face, like the kettle on the fire-place?'

'I don't think so,' Sanumaya replied. Renu noticed Karna had undone all the rope she had used. 'We don't have to take the bag,' Sudeep said, 'Renu's mother may need it for shopping.' He handed it to Renu.

'We must go,' Esther remarked, standing up. 'I'll send Sudeep to Jogbir's home to get his stuff too. Then Karna will take the bedding to our men in police custody.'

'I'll do anything else you say,' Karna pleaded, 'but please don't ask me to face my pastor again. Oh, how can I come to church now?'

'Walking on your two feet,' Esther answered, more irritated than before. 'The devil has really got hold of you. If you continue brooding on what's happened, soon he'll make you totally useless.'

'Yes, Karna *dai*, please stop. God will work all things for our good,' Sudeep added.

'Keep on praying to *Yesu*, Renu,' Esther counselled. 'You can help your father best by praying.'

'I shall,' Renu tried to sound cheerful. 'I'll pray for our pastors and Jogbir *dai* too.'

'Good girl,' Esther replied, 'you have cheered me up as well.'

'Don't worry, Renu,' Sudeep butted in awkwardly. 'We're suffering together. I feel for your father as for mine.' He had struck the right note again. Renu felt tears well up, but controlled herself. Sanumaya looked at Esther, and folded her hands in a *namasthe*. With her hands in the same position she turned to Sudeep and Karna.

'*Namasthe*,' came the response. Esther led the way.

Renu watched the group walk away solemnly from her courtyard. Karna followed Esther. Sudeep lagged behind. He appeared reluctant to depart from Renu's presence. She watched Sudeep turn around furtively three times. She heard Mother climb up the ladder, but continued watching Sudeep. He walked on sadly. Poor thing, she thought, he's come all the way from Darjeeling to see his father arrested. At the bend, Sudeep turned around and waved. Renu waved back.

'Renu, I want you to come with me,' Sanumaya sounded excited. 'Let's go to the *Pradhan Panch*.'

'Why?'

'I believe he can save Father.'

'What makes you think so?'

'Well, his wife Mohini gets along quite well with me. The way to the husband's heart is always through the wife. I could persuade her to coax her husband to help us.'

'I doubt it,' Renu answered, 'but I'll go with you.'

'Please do come,' Sanumaya pleaded needlessly. 'You can make my request stronger. The *Pradhan Panch* may also give us some more details.'

'I won't change my dress,' Renu said. 'This looks clean enough.'

'As you wish,' Sanumaya replied, and started to lock the door.

The *Pradhan Panch*'s house lay further up the hill. This suited his duty well. As the headman, he was nicknamed 'the king of the village'. From the elevated position of his house, he could survey the entire village below him. His 'queen' even noted who quarrelled with whom; and, regardless of the disgust of the villagers, reported them to her husband. However, Renu had another cause to detest her. The 'king' still had another wife, Phulmati.

'Do you think the woman who didn't pity her leprous predecessor will take pity on us now?' Renu asked Mother.

'Oh, forget that,' Sanumaya replied. 'Presumably Phulmati didn't have the luck to continue as the *Pradhan Panch*'s wife. Otherwise, why did the gods make her leprous?'

'But the doctors had healed her,' Renu protested. 'After eight months at the hospital in Kathmandu, they sent her home with a year's supply of medicine, and a certificate saying she couldn't infect others. Her husband should've known better, but he refused to believe it.'

'I heard Mohini say that the law allows a husband with a leprous wife to marry another,' Sanumaya added.

'She knows all the laws that justify her seduction of the *Pradhan Panch!* Poor man, he didn't realise how cunning this daughter of a shopkeeper could be. Each time he went to buy something, Mohini cast her spell on him.'

'Don't only blame Mohini.' Sanumaya took the side of her potential benefactor. 'We heard the *Pradhan Panch* say he needed a woman without the stigma of the disease!'

'Mohini seduced a man old enough to be her father. The *Pradhan Panch* had no choice but to take her home,' Renu pointed out.

'Phulmati didn't have the luck. Fate didn't allow it,' Sanumaya philosophised again.

'Not fate but cruelty! She persuaded her husband to push out Phulmati to the barn,' Renu continued. 'Mohini didn't manage to expel Phulmati's children, but she's suffered ever since. She has to cook and eat separately. Gradually, her children grew ashamed of their own mother!'

'How do you know that?' Sanumaya asked incredulously.

'At school the other children used to tease them, "Son of a leper! Daughter of a leper!" How well I remember the taunts.' Renu stared into space as she recalled the scenes. 'Now, Mohini nurses a son of her own. Why should she care for her step-children at all?'

'Renu, when Father returns home, I'll never treat him the way I did,' Sanumaya said, changing the subject.

'Why should you? He's stopped drinking and beating you long ago. When he got home drunk, you'd always offer him rice. Now you cook *dhindo* which he finds so hard to push down his throat. He hasn't complained.' Sanumaya listened to her in silence. 'In spite of the fact that other men laughed at him, he even went to fetch water. He's taken the cattle out whenever he could,' Renu said in her father's defence.

'They say people do stupid things before deteriorating.'

Sanumaya paused. 'I've behaved very foolishly.'

'Well, Esther and Sudeep told you to forget the past, didn't they?'

'They actually said that to Karna, but the advice could also apply to me. What the pastor's wife said impressed me a lot. How can she actually feel glad that the police have locked up her husband?'

'She told you the reason', Renu replied. 'She feels happy that Father has someone to talk to. Our pastor can comfort him. She obviously thinks about Father much more than her own husband.'

'Christians are so strange!' shrugged Sanumaya. 'I can't understand it. Perhaps Father was growing as thoughtful and selfless as the pastor's wife. I prevented him.'

'No one prevented him,' Renu replied. 'You didn't cause his arrest.'

'I hope I didn't,' answered Sanumaya. 'When Father returns I'll stop tormenting him. I promise.'

'We have to get him out of jail first.' Renu brought her mother down to earth.

Renu saw Mohini Tamang spy them from the stone fence of her courtyard.

'How lovely!' Mohini shouted. 'What a privilege to have mother and daughter sanctify our home together!' Renu did not like the flattery, but remained quiet.

'You'll think we've polluted your home when you realise why we've come,' Sanumaya answered.

'Never,' replied Mohini. 'I always look forward to your visits.'

On reaching the courtyard, Renu realised Mohini had spread out the wheat to dry. On the verandah, in a giant cradle, her baby son snored peacefully. Quite forgetting that she had shouted at them a few seconds ago, Mohini laid her right forefinger on her lips to enjoin silence, and led them away to the western corner towards the stone fence. She went and brought a straw mat. 'Preparing wheat for the mill,' Mohini said. 'Ganesh's father likes *chapatis* all the time.'

'Renu's father wants nothing made from flour,' Sanumaya put in. 'He'll eat rice all his life if he can. The fields produce wheat and maize too. What can I do?'

'Ganesh's father is also fussy,' Mohini shrugged to indicate the hard times she had with her husband. 'What brings you here today?' Renu felt relieved as the conversation showed signs of getting to the point.

'I've come to make a plea on behalf of Renu's father. You must've heard that the police have arrested him?'

'Arrested him? My god, no. When did that happen?' Mohini looked genuinely surprised.

'Please don't pretend,' Sanumaya pleaded. 'Ganesh's father must've told you everything.'

'He doesn't tell me things as he used to,' Mohini confessed. 'Now that I've given him a son, perhaps he doesn't feel the need to. Men are like that. Tell me what happened.'

'I've heard it second hand. Evidently, when Renu's father went to the river this morning, the police came, and arrested the entire group.'

'Now I remember,' Mohini turned her gaze at Sanumaya. 'Didn't you come yesterday to ask Ganesh's father to arrest your husband?'

'No,' Sanumaya choked, 'I wanted the *Pradhan Panch* to use the police to deter Renu's father, not to arrest him! Oh, how could I possibly say such a thing?' Renu looked aghast.

'Ask yourself,' Mohini replied. 'You came in a totally different mood yesterday. People can change overnight!' Mohini stood up, walked to the wheat, and stirred it with her feet.

Renu saw her mother sulking with both hands on her chin and realised where she had come after beating her the day before. Mohini returned to the straw mat. Sanumaya began her second bout of pleading. 'Can't you do anything?'

'I don't even know what happened this morning. Ganesh's father left home early. His rice has turned cold on the fireplace. I'll ask him when he gets back.'

'Please do,' Sanumaya begged. 'How shall I live with Renu's father in jail?'

'Yesterday, things were different, weren't they? You said you'd rather have your husband in jail than in the church!'

'I did, I did,' Sanumaya admitted. 'But I only asked Ganesh's father to deter Renu's father, not to arrest him!'

'Well, you should've spoken more carefully.'

'Mother made a foolish mistake. Please tell *Pradhan Panch ba* to help,' cried Renu, trying to express her mother's thoughts.

Mohini Tamang stood up. Renu realised the implication. The 'queen' did not feel the need of continuing the conversation any further. Sanumaya turned her mournful eyes on Renu, and addressed the *Pradhan Panch*'s wife once more.

'I feel ashamed to ask, but I've no choice. Could you lend me three hundred rupees? I could pay it back after the rice harvest. I don't know what my husband may need in prison.'

'Of course, ask me things I can do; and I'll do them.' Mohini sounded apologetic, and entered her house. Renu did not like her mother's sudden request for money, but understood the desperation. Mohini returned with notes crumpled in her right hand. 'I really hope you won't have to use it,' Mohini sympathised. 'Ganesh's father may manage to get him out.'

'We surely hope so,' Sanumaya mumbled.

Mohini did not sit down again, but handed the green notes to Sanumaya, who stood up to receive them.

Another strange silence prevailed on the path back home. Renu meditated on what she had heard. Sanumaya held the notes in her grip for a long time.

'Put the money away,' Renu advised. 'You may drop it and the wind may blow it over the cliff.'

'Yes, of course,' answered Sanumaya. 'I don't seem to be thinking straight any more. The wind could blow the money off the cliff . . . Thinking of the cliff, I came here first yesterday.'

'What?' Renu looked at her mother then at the cliff.

'I wanted to throw myself down, and leave the cares of the house to you two Christians. When I looked down, I lost my nerve. Then I went to Mohini. The *Pradhan Panch* had just returned from an errand somewhere. So I talked to him. Now I realise I should've followed my first impulse.'

'Don't say such a thing, Mother,' Renu chided her and thought of her prayers for her mother the day before.

'Now, how can I continue to live in the village? People will say I have betrayed my husband . . . Renu, do you believe that I asked the *Pradhan Panch* to arrest your father?'

'No, I don't,' Renu replied. 'Father flatly refused to give up worshipping *Yesu*. I wonder if the *Pradhan Panch* took his revenge for the rebuff he received.'

'My *nani*,' replied Sanumaya, 'then I can live and face the world.'

***

Renu heard someone knocking at the door. In the flicker of the kerosine lamp, she ran to it.

'*Nani*, I would like to talk to you and your mother,' the voice said from outside. Renu opened the door still not recognising the caller.

'*Pradhan Panch ba*,' Renu exclaimed, and folded her hands in greeting.

'How can I explain what has happened?' The *Pradhan Panch* started to speak, still standing. Sanumaya offered him the low wooden stool that Mahila preferred to sit on.

'The policemen either tricked me or they did things damned slowly, the bastards,' the *Pradhan Panch* said looking at Sanumaya. 'After you talked to me yesterday, I had some business down the river. So I met the policemen across the bridge. I told them what you'd said.'

'What did I say?' Sanumaya asked feebly.

'That they'd make Mahila a Christian in the morning. You didn't know what time it would be. So, I told the two constables to wait till I got there. Then, I planned to go to the scene with the policemen before Mahila and party arrived. I thought they'd all run away when they saw the two police. Things didn't go as I planned.'

'What happened?' an emotionless Sanumaya asked.

'The bastards didn't stop for me. They were too clever, and waited till they had already made Mahila a Christian. They arrested the whole lot, no doubt to coax money out of them!'

Totally overwhelmed by all that she had heard that day, Renu kept looking down at the fire-place.

'They thought they would each get a medal or something! Everything went wrong.' The *Pradhan Panch* slapped his forehead in desperation. Renu remained dumb.

'We went to your home this evening,' Sanumaya ventured.

'My wife told me. So, I came as soon as possible.'

'Only you can release Renu's father now.'

'You don't know how powerful even an ordinary constable in uniform is. They call me the 'king of the village', but the real power lies with the police. They receive pay from another king, the king of the country.'

'Surely, you can do something. After all, Renu's father lives in your village.'

'He's my nephew as well. I tried to persuade him to give up this madness. I scolded him in front of police officers. He didn't budge one bit.'

'Let him continue as a Christian,' Sanumaya pleaded, 'but please do something to get him out. Have pity on my daughter and myself, two women living alone in the house.'

'I'll try my best,' the *Pradhan Panch* assured her. 'I too will have problems showing my face in the village. Everyone will say I caused the arrest. The police have already made a big issue of it. They say my loyalty didn't even spare my own relative. They want to make me responsible for the whole affair.' The *Pradhan Panch* brooded for a while. Then he added dolefully, 'I've betrayed my nephew!'

CHAPTER
SEVEN

FATHER'S DIARY

For Renu and Sanumaya it was the fourth day of agony. On that ill-fated Sunday evening no one could persuade Karna, who had concluded that he could never face his pastor, to take the items the prisoners needed. The only news both had of Mahila was what Dambar had told them.

The arrest had drawn mother and daughter closer than ever before. For the first two days, both thought that the police wouldn't dare keep the educated pastors for long. Esther thought the same and told them so. They hoped that at their release Jogbir and Mahila would come out too. The pastor's wife was torn between doing something to get those arrested free and avoiding any rash action that would irritate the police and harden them. Therefore, she advised the course of action that most churches in Nepal are obliged to take – to pray and wait. However, it was Wednesday already. No matter what, Renu and Sanumaya would visit Mahila the next day, and they'd do so without telling Esther.

Renu went to the cattle shed to make sure the animals had fodder for the night. In a few minutes she would light the kerosine lamp, and start the fire for the evening meal. Mother had already milked the cow for that evening. She patted the small calf on its head. It turned its big eyes towards her, and wanted to lick her. 'You don't have any worries, do you?' Renu asked the calf, as if it would speak words of comfort to her. She went out to the courtyard. To her surprise, Jogbir was standing there.

'*Namasthe dai*,' Renu greeted him. 'I can't believe I'm looking at you!' A tear rolled down her cheek.

'Don't cry,' Jogbir said. 'Everything's all right . . . You'll meet your father tomorrow.' Hearing the conversation outside, Sanumaya rushed to the courtyard. Then she ran in to bring out the straw mat. Seated, Jogbir told of his release, and gave news of the rest.

In his police report, Jogbir had mentioned that he trusted in the God of Abraham, Isaac, and Jacob. Sergeant Lal had come to their room that very evening, and told him to go home. When Jogbir had protested, the sergeant had curtly replied that he was not a Christian. Why? Because Jogbir did not worship *Yesu*, but the God of Abraham, Isaac, and Jacob! Further protests were useless. Realising that his release would mean less bail to pay, Patrus and Gangaram too had advised him to go free. Further, the sergeant had ordered Jogbir to notify the *Pradhan Panch* that the remaining three would be brought to Dhanee Gaon the next day for the villagers to testify for or against them and that his presence as the 'king of the village' was required.

'I really don't know why they released me,' Jogbir moaned. 'Perhaps they're merely using me as a messenger to the *Pradhan Panch*. Perhaps they want to impress the pastors with their kindness. I'd rather have stayed with the pastors and Mahila, and improved my Nepali reading further. You know, Pastor Gangaram was coaching me!'

'What was my father doing?' Renu asked.

'I'm glad you asked that. You've reminded me of something.' Jogbir smiled a little. Taking his right hand to his chest beneath the under-garment, he took out a copy-book. 'This is what your father was doing,' Jogbir replied with a note of pride. 'He was writing all the time. The copy-book is almost full of our story, as you'll note.'

Jogbir wanted to go home and then give the news to Esther and the *Pradhan Panch*. As he got up to leave, Renu thought she had not seen anyone sadder.

Renu asked Sanumaya if she wanted the letter read to her.

'Do it tomorrow,' Sanumaya replied. 'It'll take you quite a while to get through the copy-book, and I can't read. We haven't even started the fire for our dinner yet.'

After dinner Mother wanted to get to bed. Renu couldn't blame her. After Father had been arrested, Mother's day usually started at four in the morning. Perhaps the worry woke her up so early, perhaps nightmares. By eight in the evening, Mother was ready to doze off. Renu obediently put the kerosine lamp out, and pulled it towards her in the darkness. She did not have plans to sleep early that night, no matter how tired she was. She had to read what Father had written.

Half an hour later Renu struck a match, lit the lamp, and carefully shielded it with her hands. Mother was sound asleep, yet she would take no chances of waking her up. She put the lamp on her New Testament which she had placed on her bed for a firm surface. She made a 'mountain' of her quilt towards the side opposite Mother. From under her pillow she took out the copy-book Jogbir had given her.

> My dear Renu:
> Long ago you loved to receive my letters from Kathmandu. Those letters were short, so were my trips away from home. We've just been remanded in custody, and things look ominous. For reasons you'll know in the course of reading this letter, I doubt if I may get out of this place soon. I'm preparing for the worst. That's why I have decided to start this diary. Don't mind if what I have recorded is too long. When you've read it, hide it in a safe place. Who knows if what I've written may not be useful to future generations of Christians in our country?
>
> Sunday
> I got up when the cock crowed the second time. Sanumaya and you were sound asleep. I didn't bother to wake you up. I went to the church where the two pastors, Karna and Jogbir were waiting for me.
> During daytime, I'd have allowed a bit over an hour for the journey down to the bank of the Trisuli river. I loved to run around the hair-pin bends of the dusty track. Patrus had forbidden the use of torch lights, but the moon showed the way clearly. I found the pace too slow.
> We took the usual two hours to reach the river. I looked across the suspension bridge to a small

house with a tin roof. Bless them with sleep, I prayed, as I thought of the police sergeant and three constables probably living there. However, that morning they had already started their day's work. A kerosine lamp flickered through a small window. Having no need to cross the river, Jogbir, Gangaram, Patrus, Karna, and I turned left along the bank.

I couldn't blame Gangaram for slowing the pace of the rest of us. He had come up the hill the evening before. His ankles, knee joints, and legs, used mostly to riding a motorcycle in Kathmandu, probably ached. Gangaram hummed, 'I have decided/ to follow *Yesu*/ no turning back/ no turning back.' Strangely, the hymn warmed my heart. It must have made the pastor forget his fatigue as well.

Jogbir, with the food basket in his hand, led the way. The credit of discovering the baptismal site belonged to him. The track led through the forest on the bank of the river. He had assured Patrus the previous day that the site wasn't visible from the suspension bridge because the path again turned left along the bank. I too thought that both the bend and the forest would offer secrecy.

Gangaram complained, 'Almost seven thirty in the morning! You should have chosen a place up closer to the church, Jogbir *bhai*.'

'We've arrived,' Jogbir replied. 'Above, we just have a pond where the cattle drink. I wouldn't like to take my baptism there!' Thinking back on the disaster that befell us there, I believe Gangaram was right.

Patrus undressed quickly to his shorts. Not having prepared himself beforehand, Gangaram wrapped a towel around his waist, and disappeared behind a tree. Minutes later, I saw him emerge wearing dignified blue swimming trunks.

With Karna helping at the river, Jogbir had the lone job of getting the tea ready. He set the food basket gently on the ground. He had to make two trips close to the water to get the rocks he wanted for the fire-place.

'We've quite a cook today,' I teased him, while getting shorts on myself. 'Fortunately you've no more to do than boil the water!'

'Even that may prove impossible; I can hardly find any firewood,' he replied.

'If not, we can just have the biscuits *didi* has sent,' I suggested. Renu, if you'd come, you would have felt the note of joy that prevailed then.

I saw Karna, with three towels on his shoulder, approach the shore opposite the baptismal site. Gangaram and Patrus had already entered the water. They were waiting for me to take my place between them. I overtook Karna, and stood waist deep in the water at the allotted place, shivering more from nervousness than cold. To each question Gangaram asked, I gave a 'yes'.

'Then I baptise you in the name of the Father, the Son, and the Holy Spirit!' I felt Gangaram's hands on my forehead and back. Patrus had his hands on the back of my neck and waist. The sun shone on my eyes for a second as Patrus and Mahila ducked me backwards. I felt an eternity pass before the four hands pulled me upright again. Laying both his hands on my head, Gangaram began praying for a glorious future for me. 'Amen!' we all uttered simultaneously.

When I opened my eyes, I couldn't believe what I saw. Behind Karna stood three policemen dressed fully in their uniforms. All three carried batons, and had peculiar smiles on their faces. I recognised the sub-inspector and his friend Lal, and felt sure I had seen the third person during the church service the day before. Patrus regained his composure first.

'Just having a dip in the river,' Patrus began. 'The water's turned quite cold. You should join us for a cup of tea.'

I was amazed how simply Patrus invited the policemen. Karna turned around and paled at the same time. The gurgling flow of the Trisuli had made the footsteps of the policemen inaudible.

'We will,' answered the sub-inspector. 'Then you must come with us to our office.'

'Of course, we'll come with you,' Patrus replied in resignation.

Once out of water, Patrus led the way to the fire-place. Gangaram, Karna, I, the sub-inspector, the sergeant, and the constable followed in that order. We climbed the sloping shore up to the bank. From a distance I saw another man talking to Jogbir.

My uncle himself has joined the plot! I thought when I recognised him. Jogbir blew at the fire. The *Pradhan Panch* was trying to say something to him. The smile on Jogbir's face at Patrus' approach quickly turned to a frown. He recognised the three at the end of the line behind our pastor. The *Pradhan Panch* kept his grin, appearing like a blue fiend through the puffs of the cigarette he had just lit. Patrus, Gangaram, and I picked up the bundles of clothes we had left next to Jogbir. Each of us selected a tree to hide behind while dressing. Still combing his hair, Patrus returned to the fire-place. Gangaram came a few minutes later and asked him for the comb. Although I had dressed the quickest, I wished to remain behind the tree forever. But even dressing couldn't take a day! As casually as I could, I walked to the fire.

The kettle boiled and signalled the time for tea.

'Let's serve the sahibs first,' Patrus broke the eerie silence. Jogbir took a strainer and poured off the steaming mixture of water, sugar, tea leaves and milk into the four glasses that Esther had sent. 'Fill the kettle with water, Mahila. We need more for ourselves,' Patrus ordered me. 'Don't throw away what's left in the kettle. Just add to it.' Patrus still kept his composure. How could he do it?

I walked down to the edge of the river. The constable, who had visited our church in disguise, followed me with his eyes, then with his feet just to the bank overlooking the water. For me, running errands was preferable to sitting next to my uncle by the fire-place!

The tea hadn't softened the policemen. They still asked us to come to their office. The suspension bridge swung as the nine of us walked on it. The constable led the way. Patrus, Gangaram, I, Jogbir, Karna, Sergeant Lal, the sub-inspector, and the *Pradhan Panch* followed. I wished the crossing would last a year, but we reached the sub-station in a jiffy. I had passed it as a free man so many times before that I knew the house well. It consisted of two floors; the top had beds for the policemen and the ground floor had a room for the office and another for locking people up temporarily. A shed east of the house contained the kitchen. Another sergeant was waiting in the courtyard. When the sub-inspector arrived, he saluted him smartly. Without saying a word, the sub-inspector went in to the office. Both the sergeants and the *Pradhan Panch* followed him. We went to the wall of the courtyard, and leaned on it.

I heard discussion going on in the office, but couldn't make out what the men were saying. I saw Patrus take out his New Testament, try to read something, give up, and put the book back into the shoulder bag.

Even the Pastor can't concentrate, I thought. Patrus too began to gaze at the office door. After roughly ten minutes two other constables came out. They had a rifle each. The sub-inspector followed the constables out.

'We'll go to the Trisuli barracks for questioning,' the sub-inspector announced. 'The *CDO* too wants to see you.'

'But you said you'd only bring us to the sub-station,' Patrus replied.

'That shouldn't bother you, sirs,' the sub-inspector replied politely. 'At least we have tables and chairs in the barracks. Out here you don't even have anywhere to sit.'

'Will you only question us?' Gangaram inquired.

'Yes, when people bring complaints against anyone, we at least have to go through the formalities and note something for our records.' The sub-inspector sounded almost apologetic. 'Besides, the CDO himself has taken a keen interest in meeting the Christians.'

'Just give the right answers and there should be no problem,' the *Pradhan Panch* butted in, looking at me. As defiant as ever, I stared back.

'Let's move,' the sub-inspector ordered. 'We can talk along the way.'

The single column of khaki-dressed policemen and us with a cloth shoulder bag each proved an entertainment, more interesting than listening to transistor radios. You know that the cinema has yet to come to Trisuli. People watched us from near and far, and whispered to each other. Some had a doubtful smile, others wanted as much briefing on us as they could get from those more knowledgeable. The path led by a village school which had not yet begun for the day. On the bank above the road, children of all ages were playing. The sight of the police and us tempted them to leave their games and watch us.

'We haven't done anything wrong, friends; we've been arrested because we worship *Yesu!*' Jogbir addressed the students.

'Shut up,' the sub-inspector shouted. 'Do you want a riot?'

Teenage boys and girls, urchins wiping their noses with shirt sleeves remained quiet for a while. Then all of a sudden one lad shouted, *'Hadi!'* As if in a choir the rest joined in, *'Hadi, hadi, hadi!'* When we had left the schoolchildren behind, Gangaram asked what *hadi* meant.

'I don't know,' Patrus admitted. 'Something unpleasant, I'm sure.'

'It's a local word for dog,' I replied. 'They're calling us dogs.'

'That's probably what we look like now,' Karna suggested.

While smarting from this insult, I momentarily slid back to my army days. Not a dog, but a sergeant, one of the reputed Gurkhas fighting the Japanese in Burma! I had a *kukri* on a belt around my waist and a semi-automatic rifle in my arms. All of a sudden I turned back and pulled the trigger, 'Putt, putt, putt . . .' I saw the urchins fall from the bank to the dust of the path we trod! The thoughts appalled me. After all I had just accepted baptism and apparently washed my old self away! I looked back at the urchins. Some were still staring at us; others had wandered off. I tried to smile at them.

'We've walked an hour now, Patrus *dai*,' Gangaram said, and looked at his watch just to make sure. We arrived at the main bridge over the Trisuli. I felt a shiver go down my back. The bridge led to the market street, and uphill to the police barracks. The shopkeepers would know me.

How quickly bad news spreads! Crowds had gathered on both sides of the market street of Trisuli bazaar.

'Christians, Christians!' People whispered to each other. 'One looks like the guru from Kathmandu.' Gangaram pretended not to hear. I noted among the crowd those who had shared my drunken bouts just a few months back.

'I heard he'd turned religious,' one of them said. I sighed in relief as the cobblestones of the bazaar ended.

No more spectators now, I thought, only a few passers-by!

The cobblestones gave way to the dusty yellow track again. The uphill climb tempted me to turn back and enjoy the Trisuli river which had just a few hours ago confirmed my loyalty to *Yesu*. The water that baptised me, had it flown free or had the barrage arrested it to spin the dynamos? I saw that only a trickle of the mighty Trisuli flowed on from there.

The area where the flag of the police barracks stood lay close to the office where the police were leading us. The sentry in front of the flags looked like a statue, but even he couldn't help turning his head towards us when we entered the courtyard. He stamped a salute as soon as the sergeant and the sub-inspector appeared. At the southern edge of the courtyard stood a banyan tree with a circular bench of stones around it. The two constables from the sub-station next to the suspension bridge led us there. The green grass looked more inviting, but the summer sun of the Trisuli valley made sitting impossible. We sat facing the office where we'd seen the sergeant and the sub-inspector disappear. The two constables stood in the shade, more relaxed than the colourguard a few feet away.

'What'll happen now?' asked Gangaram.

'No idea,' Patrus answered. 'They said they'd ask us something, didn't they?'

'Call Karna Tamang!' the sub-inspector's voice yelled from the office. Both the constables ran to the door.

'One of you, husbands of cows, sit with the men,' the irritated sub-inspector ordered. 'Call Karna Bahadur Tamang.' I suppressed my laughter at the new epithet. Two months previously it was the 'son of a widow'! Karna stood up as the constable came to him. Sadly, he walked to the office in front of the sub-inspector. I watched Karna's head move in response to the different questions: up and down, sideways, sideways,

sideways . . . Karna stood erect for a few minutes. Then I heard the sub-inspector say, 'You can go home!' Karna slowly turned around. His face looked as white as that of a corpse. I wanted to catch his eye, but could not. Karna kept looking down like a *Jain* trying to avoid stepping on ants. He made a left turn to the path that led to the Trisuli bazaar. Patrus and Gangaram looked at each other totally confused.

'Perhaps they'll let all of us go home?' Gangaram suggested.

'I don't know,' said Patrus, 'Karna didn't look happy.'

Jogbir's turn came next. I watched. Jogbir answered every question by nodding sideways. A few minutes later he turned around and smiled at the two pastors and me. A constable held him by the left arm, led him to a room barely four yards away from the office, pushed him inside, shut the door, and stood in front of it.

'I'll go in next whoever they may call,' P rus told Gangaram and me.

'Call Mahila,' the sub-inspector roared again.

Patrus stood up and rushed to the constable. Puzzled, the constable led him to the office.

'Not him, you husband of a cow!' I heard the sub-inspector curse, then a gentler voice. 'I didn't call you, sir.' Gangaram and I watched. Again, the usual nods of the head. To the amazement of both of us, a policeman brought a chair for Patrus.

'You go in last, Mahila,' said Gangaram. 'Patrus and I should take responsibility for what's happened.' I had no time to protest.

'Call Mahila!' Gangaram rushed in through the door even before the constable had started to move.

'You're in a hurry?' I heard the sub-inspector say to Gangaram.

Given to frequent preaching, the pastors didn't know how to whisper their answers.

'I'm responsible for all this. I came from Kath-mandu.'

'I invited Gangaram*ji*. I'm responsible.'

'Please wait there.' I saw Gangaram sit on a wooden bench on the right side of the room.

The constable came to me even though the inspector didn't call out again. I accepted the inevitable and walked to the office door. Beside the sub-inspector at the table sat Sergeant Lal, the *Pradhan Panch*, and another man with a dark face and eyes like those of a cobra. The sub-inspector turned to me, standing in anticipation of what would happen next. Just then, I saw the officer looking beyond me to the door and standing up to salute.

I turned around. I didn't know the person who'd just entered. However, I instinctively did a *namasthe*. Patrus and Gangaram followed suit. Seeing that the sub-inspector himself fumbled about to find a chair for the newcomer, I guessed him to be someone big.

'The inspector sahib's arrived at just the right moment,' announced the sub-inspector. The inspector sat a bit behind those at the table and looked on.

'The prosecutor sahib here will ask you questions,' the sub-inspector introduced the man who reminded me of the cobra. I didn't like his looks.

'Why have you become a Christian?'

'Because *Yesu* died for my sins, and has given me heavenly life.'

'Will you have a heavenly life when we lock you up?'

'I will because *Yesu* will continue to love and comfort me.'

'Who made you a Christian?'

'I decided to follow *Yesu* on my own,' I replied. 'No one enticed me.'

'But you must have received lots of American money?'

'Never. I'd not walk around like this if I did,' I replied pointing to my simple clothes. 'I farm and keep cattle like the rest of the villagers.'

'Why have you left the religion of your forefathers?'

'No one holds on to something that doesn't help,' I replied. 'Only *Yesu* offers heavenly life.'

'You think all the rest of us non-Christians will go to hell, don't you?'

'I've no authority to say that. God will decide.'

'Do you want to return to Hinduism?'

'Never,' I answered. 'I'd rather die than desert *Yesu*.' I saw the inspector frowning.

'Why should you ask him all these questions?' the inspector asked the prosecutor. 'Roughly two months ago, this fellow beat up someone in the village and absconded. Didn't he, Modhnath?'

'Yes, sir,' replied the sub-inspector. 'Sergeant Lal went with me the morning he ran away.'

'We can settle that,' Patrus broke in. 'Mahila beat me up under the influence of drink. Things have changed. We've become friends, so we don't need to discuss this matter any more.'

'We do,' answered the inspector. 'When someone brings in a complaint, we cannot just forget about it. Why did this fellow abscond?'

'I didn't abscond,' I protested. 'These two sahibs here took two hundred rupees from me, and told me to disappear for a few days!' The *Pradhan Panch* looked straight at me, and bit his tongue in feigned amazement.

I clearly saw I had exploded a bombshell. The prosecutor turned towards Sergeant Lal and Sub-Inspector Modhnath. The inspector fixed his gaze on them both for a while, and smiled a bit. I stood uneasily.

'Strange things happen,' Inspector Kuber Singh turned philosophical. 'As long as we live we don't cease to hear of them.'

'This drunkard can say what he likes,' Modh-

nath put in a defence for the sergeant and himself.
'Neither of us would sell our honour for such a
paltry sum. We are here to question him, not he to
accuse us!'

'I served in the army,' I continued, 'and have
had contacts with the police. They take even five
rupees, let alone two hundred.' I saw Patrus
wince.

'Let's get to the point,' the prosecutor requested.

'Yes, we'd better forget the things of the past,'
the *Pradhan Panch* broke his silence. 'I asked this
so-called nephew of mine to stop his madness.
Even a mule wouldn't be that stubborn.'

'I don't need your help, uncle,' I responded.
'Perhaps I wouldn't be here if you hadn't directed
the policemen!'

'You wouldn't be here if your wife hadn't given
me the details,' the *Pradhan Panch* retorted. 'She
begged me to stop you. I meant to come with a
few constables to the river early to scare your
contingent away. However, I got up too late. Still,
nothing drastic has happened. You can go home
the moment you say you'll observe the religion of
your forefathers.' The *Pradhan Panch* looked at the
prosecutor who nodded in agreement.

'Do you want to return to your own religion
again, Mahila?' The prosecutor appeared almost to
plead with me.

'Definitely not, not after all that *Yesu* has done
for me!'

'I told you,' the *Pradhan Panch* replied,' as
stubborn as an old buffalo that insists on going to
the cliffs. A traitor!'

'Uncle, my father lost his life in Birganj during
the revolution of *two thousand and seven*. He shed
his blood to bring in democracy. I too fought
against the Japanese in Burma during the Great
War. I almost died for the honour of our country.
Just because I choose to follow *Yesu*, I can't under-

stand why you should consider me a traitor,' I said, almost gasping.

'Don't you know that we have different laws in this country?' the prosecutor asked me. 'You've full freedom to continue worshipping the gods of your forefathers.'

'But what if the gods of my ancestors couldn't help me? I'd rather die than obey a law that prevents me from worshipping my living Lord,' I retorted.

An unbearable silence followed. As if to escape from the difficult decision that lay ahead, the prosecutor lazily scribbled on the cover of his file of papers. The sub-inspector certainly looked irritated. The sergeant stared at the table he leaned on.

The prosecutor finally looked at Patrus and Gangaram. 'You, sirs, have come all the way from Kathmandu and Darjeeling to get into this trouble,' the prosecutor sounded apologetic. 'Our government doesn't forbid worshipping any deity as long as you don't disturb others. Both of you, sirs, can go free!' Gangaram looked at Patrus, then at me. I fidgeted a bit.

'Thank you, thank you indeed,' Patrus answered. 'However, we've given exactly the same answers as Mahila or Jogbir. You lock them up and tell us to go free. We'll go, but only with our companions.'

'I say the same,' chimed in Gangaram.

For a few seconds, I saw the prosecutor turn red. The inspector played with his baton, and caressed it from end to end. The sergeant stared between the heads of the two pastors. The prosecutor finally turned to one of the constables. 'All right,' he said, 'take them all in.'

'Come along, sirs,' the constable turned to us.

'A big catch!' I heard the sub-inspector mutter.

Renu, I can never forget the identification of those two pastors with us. Had they gone free, we surely would've suffered a lot worse.

The constable closed the door behind us. I had used 'maternal uncles' as a euphemism for the police many times, but now I was actually experiencing their 'hospitality'. The sight of Jogbir sitting on the wooden stocks cheered the pastors and me.

'Oh Jogbir, important guests have come. You haven't even swept the room clean!' I jested.

Patrus and Gangaram embraced Jogbir. I took my turn last.

'This room can't measure more than ten by seven feet,' Gangaram said to Patrus. I noticed our window, approximately one foot square, to the right.

'I don't like sitting in the dark. We'd better open this,' I said. 'Jogbir didn't even think of it till now. What have you been doing for the last hour?'

'I too felt pretty cheerful on my baptism day, just like Mahila now,' Jogbir replied. 'In fact I couldn't sleep the whole night for joy. To get some sleep, I got up and ate two cloves of garlic.'

'You may need four cloves to open this wretched window!' said Patrus, joining in the festivities. The small wooden pane had apparently jammed long ago into the frame. Both he and Gangaram pulled at it, but it didn't move a fraction of an inch.

'We'd better not force it in case we break it,' Gangaram said.

Gangaram knocked on the door, and asked the sentry to help. I guessed from the noise that the sentry was hitting a piece of wood with a brick through the wooden bars outside the pane. Bang, bang, bang! The stubborn window refused to open. The bangs grew louder. Finally, the sentry opened the door. 'I may lose my job if I break the window. One sergeant came by and said that no other inhabitants of this room had made a such a request before. I'll open the door instead.'

'That'll do,' Patrus replied. 'We just need some light and fresh air.'

The sentry opened the door wide. 'Just ask when you want to go to the toilet. Think of this as your own home!' he said. We waited for him to move away.

'Think of this as my own home?' laughed Patrus. 'Not until they bring Esther here too.'

'At least the chap sounds friendly. We ought to cultivate friendship with him,' Gangaram suggested as he took his seat on the old, damp mat.

Patrus and I sat too. Jogbir went back to the stocks.

'By all means cultivate his friendship, as the goat with the butcher,' Patrus replied.

'Jogbir *bhai*, you act as our "sentry" on their sentry,' I requested. I took out my notebook from my shoulder bag.

'What are you doing?' Patrus asked from his seat in the corner.

'I'd better keep a diary,' I said. 'I am going to write how the maternal uncles treat us daily. Who knows? It may be useful some day.' Jogbir moved over on the straw mat next to the door.

'When I cough,' Jogbir said, 'you'll know that your "uncle" is coming. Hide your copy-book somewhere.' The internal sentry took up his position.

The gong struck two. I wondered how we'd pass the day. Ever since we arrived at the barracks in the morning, we'd been hearing the gong ring only once every half hour. At every hour the number of peals corresponded to the time. I noticed the youthful delight of the sentry when his turn came to strike the gong.

Passing the day didn't prove problematic. Patrus suggested that we should have a time of prayer. When we had finished that, Gangaram spontaneously led out in a chorus, 'Yesterday, today, forever, *Yesu* is the same . . .' The chorus had hardly lasted a minute when the sentry rushed to stop us singing. When we didn't stop, a sergeant came.

'We don't sing all the time,' Patrus replied, 'but you can't prevent us praying and worshipping.'

'But our sahibs have locked you up precisely for that,' the sergeant protested.

'Precisely for that, we chose not to deny *Yesu* and go free,' Gangaram retorted. 'You can kill us, but you'll not stop us worshipping.' The sergeant threw up his hands in a do-whatever-you-like fashion and left.

'We'd better not irritate the sergeant any more. Let's do something else. Many people study quite a lot during times like this,' Patrus shared his bright idea. 'I'll coach Jogbir in his Nepali reading.'

Jogbir took out his New Testament from his bag. By chance, he opened up the last book, Revelation. As he read, Patrus followed in his New Testament and corrected him whenever he stumbled over a word. Gangaram and I let the words we heard sink into our hearts. Jogbir's slow reading allowed ample time.

Even prisoners have to take care of nature. The trips to the back of the house brought a contrast to the drab atmosphere in the room. I noticed Gangaram ask the sentry's permission to go out.

'A literal hell,' Gangaram exclaimed on return. Patrus and Gangaram felt the daily humiliation of going to the toilet in the open even more than I did. The police must have had at least four hundred men in the barracks. They could have made proper toilets. Perhaps prisoners have no rights to expect privacy.

Soon Gangaram and Patrus were debating the events going on in Kathmandu. Jogbir hadn't followed much of the conversation, and had quietly dozed off. My previous military background made the subject matter at least comprehensible.

'Nepal had one of the most unfortunate rever-
sals in history. Hundreds of martyrs shed blood to
bring democracy in the year *two thousand and seven*.
Ten years later this country became a one-party,
one-religion state. Back to zero! That's why we are
locked up today,' Patrus began.

'Do not talk about the past. Strange things have
happened in Kathmandu just recently,' Gangaram
continued. 'They've discovered that the former
IGP had dealings with international smuggling
gangs. They arrested him, but the corrupt officials
higher up have escaped.'

'Higher?'

'The sky's the limit, Patrus*ji*,' Gangaram
replied. 'Who knows if they haven't bugged this
room? I daren't get more specific. However,
because of all this, there's so much frustration in
the country. Most of my classmates have migrated
to the west. I should have settled there too when I
had the chance fourteen years ago. I couldn't. For
better or worse, God gave me this country. I'll
live, serve, and die here.'

'I agree. Heaven is where *Yesu* has placed you.
. . . Do you know what?' Patrus changed the
subject. 'They said they'd question us at the sub-
station next to the bridge. Instead, they brought us
out here, asked us some foolish questions, and
locked us up. They haven't even given us proper
warrants. We could die here unnoticed. At this
rate no one could hold the police officially responsible. We need warrants, don't we?'

'True,' Gangaram added. 'We need proper
warrants.'

'Right,' I chimed in. 'Without warrants they
don't even need to feed us. I know at least this
much from military experience.'

'Neither could a lawyer help us, even if we
wanted one to,' Patrus rose up.

'Wake Jogbir up, the poor cook!' Gangaram
suggested. 'By the way where did we leave the

utensils Esther sent for our tea this morning?'

'I saw the police take them away from Jogbir. They must have kept them at the sub-station near the bridge,' I responded. Jogbir woke up fully, and confirmed it.

'Well, we've lost them forever, then,' replied Patrus.

'Let's put in a complaint,' Gangaram suggested.

'No – forget it!'

We filed out one by one, and leaned against the outer wall of the room we'd just vacated.

'Sirs, get in,' the sentry pleaded.

'Not till we get proper warrants. If you want to arrest us, do it properly!' Gangaram acted as the spokesman, Patrus echoed him, I murmured the same, but Jogbir only nodded. The sentry ran to the same sergeant who, hours before, had requested us to refrain from singing.

'I'd better go to the sub-inspector about this,' the sergeant said.

'And bring the *CDO* too. They said he wanted to see us. What deceit!' Gangaram sounded furious.

The sergeant didn't reply. In contrast to the constables who had their uniforms on, the sergeant wore a red shirt, brown shorts, and thonged sandals on his feet. I laughed to myself as I saw this sloppy figure running to call his superior. Adamant, we stood against the wall.

Neither the sub-inspector nor the *CDO* came. Instead we heard the noise of a typewriter clattering away in the office. Uniformed and casually dressed policemen went back and forth. I wondered what the flurry was about. After about half an hour, the typing stopped. Another sergeant entered the office. He still had his uniform on. I knew him only too well.

'Mahila Tamang,' Sergeant Lal called from the office door. I approached the policemen. Lal handed me a piece of paper, and asked me to sign it. I did it in a jiffy. Then I signed another paper which the police kept. I walked back to my three friends, and from a distance watched them repeat the process. Finally, Gangaram held his piece of paper.

'We should keep this carefully,' advised Gangaram. 'Otherwise what evidence have we?'

'Let's go in now,' Patrus suggested. We filed into the room one by one, and laughed for a while. Jogbir took his place by the door.

The gong struck seven when I heard a familiar voice talking to the sentry. I looked out, but saw only the back of the newcomer and the *doko* he had obviously carried. The man turned towards the door.

'Dambar Tamang's come. He has brought a *doko* full of stuff too.' I must've sounded like a child with a basket of presents. The other three crept quickly to the door. The sentry led Dambar to our room.

'*Namasthe*,' Dambar, folding his two palms in greeting, met the four pairs of eyes that gazed at him. '*Pastorni ama* sent me with all the bedding and things you may need.'

'I've orders to check each item you give them,' the sentry addressed Dambar.

'Check them in front of us,' Patrus requested. Dambar pulled out the items one by one.

'Bedding for Mahila *dai*. I think Renu has put a towel and soap inside. Pastor *dai's* sleeping bag. Jogbir's bedding and bag. This nice travel bag must belong to pastor *dai* from Kathmandu!' Gangaram almost dived for his red airline bag with pockets on all sides.

'Now, I can stay here for ever!' Gangaram exclaimed.

'Don't speak too soon,' Patrus cautioned. The sentry went through the bags and took out different items.

'We'll have to keep these with us in the office.

You can take them when you go home.' Exhibiting razor blades, shavers, and a nail cutter in his palms, the sentry walked out.

'Who told you about the arrest?' Patrus asked, turning to Dambar.

'How fast bad news travels,' Dambar moaned. 'Karna came home weeping, then within an hour all the village was buzzing with excitement.'

'They must have been pleased,' Patrus added.

'Sadly, most of them were. Some noted the change that had come about in Mahila's life, and asked what the police were really after in arresting him.'

'We'll know that in due time, Dambar *bhai*,' replied Patrus.

'All of you will have to pray very seriously for Karna,' Dambar requested. 'He cried three or four times saying that he had betrayed the Lord and that he couldn't face other Christians any more. We tried to comfort him. He even wanted to return here and seek re-arrest. *Pastorni ama* managed to dissuade him from that.'

'Poor Karna. Tell him that we continue to love him all the same. He should try to forgive himself,' Patrus added.

'He has prayed to the Lord for forgiveness many times. He just remembers the verse from the Bible about the unforgivable sin, and thinks he's done it.'

'Yes, the gospel of Mark chapter three,' Gangaram recalled. 'That verse has caused agony to thousands throughout the history of the church. However, there *Yesu* wasn't saying it to sorrowful souls like Karna, but to the unrepentant scribes from Jerusalem. You should sit with Karna, and point out verse 22 to him, Dambar *bhai*. *Yesu* doesn't impute eternal sin to one who cries in repentance three or four times a day.'

'I shall try,' answered Dambar.

'Dambar *bhai*, you should go home now,' Patrus

advised. 'The police will object if you remain too long with us. Better short visits than none at all. Give them the news that our Lord has kept us rejoicing. Who knows? Jogbir may read Nepali better than I when we come out! With his farm work not bothering him here, he can spend the whole day reading. Tell them to keep praying.'

I felt strangely sad as Dambar put the ropes into the *doko*, and walked out of the door. I saw Jogbir and the two pastors spread out their beds. I did the same with the bedding you, dear Renu, had sent. The darkness increased the depression I'd already begun to feel.

By the time the gong struck eight, electric lights illuminated most rooms of the barracks. The dynamo on the Trisuli river had bestowed its generosity on all but us.

'Why no light here?' Jogbir asked. I sensed his depression too.

'The same reason why they took our shaving kits and razor blades away,' Gangaram replied. 'People locked up in a cell like this can do any-thing to themselves. The police don't want suicides on their hands, do they?'

'They should give us a kerosine lamp then.'

'Why don't you ask?'

Jogbir called out to the sentry who after a while returned with a flickering, burning object in his hand.

When meal time finally came, I found myself jumping up first. We used the same water spout in the ground that the ordinary policemen used. I noticed that they had a bathroom, after all; but it was only for the inspector, his wife and children, and those nearest in rank to him. The police had already eaten. The cook at the kitchen handed us a plate each, certainly belonging to other policemen. I took mine and washed it just to make sure it was thoroughly clean. Jogbir followed my example, and offered to clean the plates the pastors received. As expected, the cook gave us plenty of rice, but just a little bit of onion and potato curry. To ensure easier swallowing, I asked for as much *dahl* as possible. Strangely, I found I preferred the spinach curry and the *dhindo* Sanumaya and you cooked. A tear trickled down my cheek, but I stealthily wiped it away. The cook emptied the last bit of *dahl* on Jogbir's plate. I swallowed the dry chunks of rice, and felt myself choking on them. On our way back to the cell, I belched at the satisfaction of having eaten as much as I could.

We were about to turn off the kerosine lamp when the sentry came again to the door. The voice had changed and also the person. He announced that the quartermaster of the barracks wanted to pay us a visit.

'Of course,' replied Patrus, 'whenever he pleases.' I'd already seen the quartermaster standing at the door. As soon as Patrus spoke, he entered.

'Just to see if you're all comfortable,' the quartermaster stated the alleged purpose of his visit. I noticed the sweaty bald patch on his head. The officer stank of alcohol.

'Our friends brought us some bedding from home. We feel quite comfortable, sahib,' Jogbir answered.

'I can still get you some blankets and overcoats if you want,' the quartermaster suggested.

My former military days! The great war! I remembered how as a guard in my green overcoat I'd paced up and down the quarters in the Naga hills!

'I'd like to have an overcoat,' I asked softly. The others echoed my request.

'All right,' agreed the quartermaster. 'I'll send four overcoats and four blankets.'

'Very kind of you,' replied Patrus.

'Anything you need, just ask,' the quartermaster urged as he left. The sentry came to the door and looked in again.

'I'll have to lock the door.'

'Please keep it open,' Gangaram requested. 'The last sentry couldn't open the window. It's stuffy, and we need some fresh air. We won't run away.'

'All right,' agreed the sentry, 'call out when you want to go to the toilet.' While my friends either prayed or meditated on the bizarre events of the day, I blew at the kerosine lamp and extinguished it.

Monday

At about two in the morning, I felt my body itching all over. The special atmosphere of the Trisuli valley ensured that mosquitoes didn't thrive there, and so for a while I remained non-plussed. Then my suspicion centred on the green overcoat I had used for extra insulation against the damp floor. Lice and ticks raced over my body. I turned over onto my stomach, and started to pray. My mind wandered to you and your mother, the *Pradhan Panch* and the folks back in our village. I remembered *Yesu's* command to pray for one's persecutors. May God bless those who rejoice and gloat over my plight, I mumbled to myself. However, bitterness overcame me as I focused on the *Pradhan Panch,* my distant uncle. I reached out to the regions on my back where the vermin ran, and scratched where it irritated.

The gong woke me up as it struck four. Shame on me, I scolded myself, I fell asleep while praying! I tried to concentrate on *Yesu* again, but found it impossible. My mind replayed different scenes from Trisuli valley, Dhanee Gaon, and Dhading. I surmised what my relatives far and near would say. The stigma of spending time in police custody or jail would remain for ever. I had committed no crime. Like numerous politicians, I tried to regard the experience as a medal! However, I could do that only after attaining freedom. More pertinent right then was the matter of the toilet which I had determined to use before anyone else did. I stirred about a bit.

'Are you awake already?'

'Bugs are crawling all over me,' I replied to Patrus. 'I've no choice.'

'We made a mistake in accepting the overcoats,' Patrus confessed. 'They looked so inviting. We should've realised that lots of people would've worn them before us, and nobody would've washed them.'

'Do you want to go out, Mahila? Do you need my torch light?' Gangaram offered. So far only Jogbir remained silent. I wished I too could sleep, quite oblivious to the vermin.

'I'll use it, thank you,' I responded.

'Leave it next to the door, so that whoever wants to go out may take it.'

I heard the gong sound once.

Realising that dawn would arrive within an hour and a half, I walked out, and notified the sentry of my desire. The sentry showed me the drum which held water exclusively for anal cleansing.

'Do not dip this can into the other drum,' the sentry warned. 'Take water out and fill the bottle.'

Noting that the bottle had a broken neck, I followed the instruction carefully. I grasped it at the middle to avoid cutting myself, and walked behind the room where we had just spent the night. The bank went down through a series of terraced fields to the small stream down below. On the other side stood similar terraces and banks. I imagined the urchins bringing their cattle for grazing during the day.

At least the night affords privacy, I thought as I turned the torch light off. When my eyes adjusted to the darkness, I saw the sentry watching me from a distance.

My companions had also realised the advantage of going to the toilet before dawn. As I entered the room, Jogbir asked for the torch light. Then Patrus followed him. Finally, Gangaram. I pitied the latter the most. He must've longed for the facilities of his modern home in Kathmandu!

The sun had begun to cast its golden rays when I saw policemen walking back and forth towards the kitchen. They carried cups of tea and two *puris* each. From my military days I remembered that menu as the standard early morning diet for soldiers. The police had the same. My mouth watered for the *puris*, and I wondered when the sentry would ask us to walk towards the kitchen. I waited in vain. The gong struck eight. Just then I saw a policeman in ordinary clothes walk towards our door.

'I've come to ask if you'd like me to buy tea for you all.'

'Won't we have breakfast with all the other policemen?' Gangaram inquired.

'No, you'll get your rice meals in the morning and evening, but you'll have to buy everything else.'

'All right then, how much money will you need?'

'Two rupees for four cups.'

Patrus offered to pay, and handed the constable a five-rupee note. After he left, Gangaram shook his head.

'We praised the quartermaster's generosity yesterday. How could we know he had another stingy side? He can't even offer us a morning cup of tea!'

'I wonder if they give meals to others as they have to us,' I added. 'When the police locked up some men from my village, I remember their families brought food to them.'

'That happened in Kathmandu too when they took two brothers from our church. They kept them three days. Our friends could eat only what we provided,' Gangaram confirmed.

'Prisoners whom the court has convicted get meagre rations, but usually not those in custody,' I replied. 'We've received lunch and dinner only because you two pastors share our fate.'

'Obviously, the government has allocated funds for feeding those in custody too. The rascals even exploit them!'

Gangaram looked longingly towards the kitchen which supplied the breakfast policemen carried to their quarters.

Our own breakfast arrived a few minutes later. 'You need this to go with your tea,' the constable said as he placed a small kettle, four glasses, and a packet of biscuits in front of us. Patrus received the change.

'By the way, the nearest shop we have belongs to a *Brahmin*. He doesn't take back glasses used by people of low caste,' the constable explained.

'Does he break them then?' Gangaram could be excused for his sarcasm. The constable did not reply.

'Could you wash at least those two glasses?' The constable turned to Jogbir and me. 'I'll come to take them in about half an hour.'

'We'll wash them all,' Gangaram replied in disgust.

'No need to,' the constable assured them.

'The shopkeeper will naturally relegate our two Tamang friends here to low caste. What of us? Doesn't he consider all Christians the same?' asked Gangaram.

'Then wash all four glasses and the kettle too,' the constable requested cheerfully. 'Why offend odd people like this *Brahmin*? After all, we'll need to buy tea from him as long as you remain in this room.'

'Tell me one thing,' Patrus asked. 'Will the shopkeeper accept money which we low-caste people have touched?'

With a grin, the constable left the room.

The packet had seventeen biscuits. All agreed that the youngest should have five and the rest four. Jogbir easily qualified for the extra one. I looked forward to the rice meal in a few hours' time.

The constable came to take away the kettle and the glasses which I had washed.

'We have a holiday today, Lord Buddha's birthday!'

'Oh,' replied Gangaram. 'Then we'll have plenty of peace to look forward to. Buddha taught and preached peace.'

'And fun too,' the constable replied. 'Some of my friends who have families nearby went home yesterday.' I watched the constable leave with the utensils. In the course of rinsing the glasses and the kettle, I had returned with my face washed. The three others decided to visit the tap.

I took my New Testament out, and began to read Revelation mainly because I'd seen Jogbir's interest in the last book of the Bible. However, I didn't have quiet for long. The sentry I'd seen the day before came along with another man who carried a hammer and a chisel.

'We have to get this small window open so that we can shut your door at night,' the policeman said. 'We left it open yesterday, but we mustn't do it again. Where have the others gone?'

'To the tap to wash their faces,' I replied.

While his friend went towards the window, the former sentry went out to make sure.

'I can see them at the tap,' he said. 'But, tell them to go one by one next time.' I nodded in agreement. The two went at the window, one from inside the room, the other from outside. The hammering and the chiselling proved too much for the age-weary wooden structure. The pane opened, and blessed the room with a bit more light. I began the second chapter of the book of Revelation.

Patrus, Gangaram, and Jogbir returned. Jogbir held the soap which had become common to all of us. They all had towels on their shoulders.

'Sorry, we're back so late,' Patrus apologised. 'We found the inspector's wife watering her garden. My! Didn't she take a long time? When she finished, the water had gone down to a trickle. It must have stopped flowing altogether by now!'

'The sentry we saw yesterday brought along a fellow to open the window. We have more light now,' I reported. 'He says they'll keep the door shut at night. He also warned us to go to the tap one by one.'

'Accepted,' Gangaram nodded. 'Oh, how refreshing to wash!'

'I didn't warn Mahila yesterday, but I will now,' Patrus began, sitting down on the straw mat. 'Never mention again that you bribed the sergeant and the sub-inspector.'

'But I did bribe them,' I replied. 'Only then did they advise me to disappear for a few days.'

'I know, I know,' Patrus answered. 'But they have us in their clutches now. They can plot anything against us. I saw both the sergeant and the sub-inspector very embarrassed in front of their boss. That may not bode well for our future.'

'Yes,' I admitted.

'In future questioning, don't even mention that,' Patrus warned me again. 'The police here can make black white and white black. We should take all precautions.'

After all the policemen had eaten, we received an invitation to walk to the kitchen for our morning meal. Dinner would be twelve hours away! I encouraged our friends to eat as much as possible.

'I find it difficult to swallow dry rice with too little vegetable and *dahl*,' Gangaram confessed, 'but I'll try.'

Buddha's birthday!

Another excuse for the policemen to gamble, I thought. I lay down to meditate on my bed after the heavy rice meal. According to my reckoning, the police had a holiday every day. Most of the running around had to do with maintaining the population in the barracks. They didn't have a parade-ground, and thus had an excuse not to exercise.

'We'll read again, after you rest a bit,' Patrus said to Jogbir. I got up and began to scribble in my diary. Just then Jogbir noted Sergeant Lal approaching the door, and coughed. I folded the copy-book in half and hid it under my thigh.

'We'll have the official police questioning today in about half an hour,' Lal said. 'After that you can go and sit under the banyan tree.' The sergeant smiled and left.

'They don't celebrate Buddha's birthday, do they?' Gangaram asked. 'Why the hurry with our case?'

My turn came first. They led me to the stone stairs adjacent to the office. I climbed up. To my surprise, I didn't see two rooms as on the ground floor. The single room stretched the entire expanse under its long roof. A striped brown cloth carpet lay pressed by the chairs and the people on them. Besides the prosecutor, Sergeant Lal, and Sub-Inspector Modhnath, I saw two men I didn't recognise. One of them had a pen and sheets of Nepali paper. With a small knife, he cut the sheets to the size he wanted. The other person, who sat with folded arms, had an air of importance. The prosecutor pointed out a chair for me.

The questions sounded very similar to the ones I had answered the previous day. In fact I wondered if they had repeated the process only to get the details in black and white. When the scribe had finished writing, he read out the contents. I nodded in agreement that the scribe had recorded the facts accurately. The scribe then indicated where I should sign.

My friends repeated the process I'd just finished. When Gangaram had gone to face the police, we meditated on what we'd just said and how the police or court would use the evidence. I'd emphasised my respect for Hinduism. Fortunately, the question of the bribe the two police officers had taken didn't even arise.

Gangaram returned quite jubilant. 'Did you all get a cup of tea?' Gangaram looked at us as if we had kept some secret from him. All of us shook our heads.

'Well, I did! They asked me a lot of questions. The prosecutor wanted to know why the Protestants and the Catholics don't get along together. I had to repeat the story of Martin Luther and the Reformation to enlighten them about it! The prosecutor also advised me to come for a chat whenever we wanted to tell him something.'

'This smells fishy,' Patrus said.

'Of course. What would we want to tell the prosecutor anyway?' Gangaram looked puzzled.

'How much money we will give him, of course!' Patrus replied. Jogbir nodded his head vigorously. 'Mahila says he received a strange message this morning while they broke open this window,' Patrus continued. 'The sentry assured him we'd go free if we just threw a few thousand rupees. I feel they want to grab our purse more than protect Hinduism.'

'Yes, yes, I'll have to be wary of their future offers of tea,' Gangaram felt his doubts had cleared.

'This morning the sergeant said we could go out to the tree. Should we go?' put in Jogbir, changing the subject.

'Ask the sentry, Jogbir,' Patrus advised. The sentry agreed. We rushed to the banyan tree like calves let loose from the pegs that tether them.

The banyan tree offered a good view of the
Trisuli river. As my companions opened up their
New Testaments, I just wanted to watch it flow. I
envied the freedom it enjoyed. I wondered if the
water that had baptised me the day before had
already reached India. Gracious and generous, the
river spun the giant turbines that churned out so
much electricity. Unfortunately, Dhanee Gaon,
just three hours' walk away, still had to manage
with kerosine lamps. Huge cables carried the
power to Kathmandu. Exploitation everywhere, I
thought, our district has the resources but others
use it up!

In the distance on the bank of the river, I saw an
elderly man and a small child fishing with cane
rods and strings. I waited to see if they'd pull out
a catch. They lifted their rods many times, but
only the hooks with the bait appeared. I didn't
mourn at the anglers' bad luck. Rather I sympathised with the fish. If they took the bait, they'd
share a fate worse than mine! The fishermen got
tired of the spot and moved further down the
river. I must have watched people fishing a
hundred times before. Never before did it speak
so much to me.

Rather than lapse into a daydream, I decided to
read the New Testament. I again flipped the pages
to the beginning of Revelation chapter 2. I came to
verse 10: 'Do not fear what you are about to suffer.
Behold, the devil is about to cast some of you into
prison, that you may be tested, and you will have
tribulations *ten* days. Be faithful until death, and I
will give you the crown of life.'

All of a sudden, I felt my heart warm. Only ten
days, I guessed, and we'll go free! I looked up into
the clear blue sky. An eagle made huge circles. It
didn't flap its wings. It surveyed the creatures
below and floated lazily. The regality and the
wanton freedom of the king of the birds impressed
me. Beyond the reach of stones or bullets, it could

go to sleep in the air!

I remembered the end of the verse I'd just read. Faithful until death? The crown of life? I wished I could decide which part applied to me. The exact knowledge of God's will proved difficult to this young Christian, barely two days old!

We didn't want to leave the tree and its shade. We went into our room now and then for our Bibles or pens. The same constable of the morning bought us our afternoon tea. The sentry under the flag felt relaxed with us. The tree too had begun to symbolise freedom, however limited.

Towards the evening, I saw a line of people approaching the tree. In front walked a policeman. Two middle-aged men and a haggard woman followed. Then came three more policemen. I pointed out the sight to others. They all watched.

'More company,' Gangaram said. 'I wonder what they've done.'

The group approached closer and closer. The policeman at the head of the line directed them to the office door. On second thoughts, the other policeman motioned the men and the woman to sit on the grass and wait. In the office, heels stamped in salute. Voices echoed back and forth. The policeman who had led the group came out, and took the three to the room next to the one we occupied. Some policemen slept in the same room. Didn't they fear that the three would attempt an escape? Or did the new arrivals appear too weary to do so?

Jogbir mentioned that the police were killing two goats for dinner. It seemed odd on Buddha's birthday. The sage wouldn't have hurt a fly! Evidently, with all the manpower the barracks had, they found it much cheaper to buy goats and slaughter them than to purchase meat from town. My mouth watered profusely. I couldn't concentrate on the New Testament I tried to read. I decided I'd beg for a lot of gravy, and push in as much rice as possible. In sheer anticipation of the meal, I started whistling cheerfully.

Dinner time came later than the previous day. The gong had struck ten. As we walked to the kitchen, we saw policemen standing in rows. One officer gave instructions. Evidently, he wanted people to bring various things. The items – pins, nettles, chilli powder, sticks – amazed me. Trying not to appear nosy, we made a bee line for our dinner.

'I'm late tonight,' the cook said. 'I had to prepare a separate meal for you.' We didn't understand. Full of anticipation I washed the plates and handed them to the cook. He dished out mountains of rice on each plate. With the ladle he poured out two helpings of *dahl*. My heart ached as I kept on watching. The cook gave us a helping each of potato and onion curry, but no meat!

'What little respect I had for the police has vanished completely,' Gangaram, back in our room, said to Patrus. 'Poor Jogbir, he expected meat on his plate tonight!'

'I think we all did,' Jogbir replied, blushing. 'We could smell it from the kitchen.'

'Man does not live by meat alone,' Gangaram added, striking a serious note.

'Nevertheless, you'd survive better if you had it today!' laughed Patrus. I nodded in agreement.

'Next time they kill a goat we'll buy a kilo of it,' Patrus assured us. 'Jogbir can cook for us.'

'I will,' replied Jogbir, 'if only to make the police jealous!'

The second night of police hospitality approached. We talked about things we never had leisure for in the past. Jogbir and I told jokes, but they soon turned a bit dry. Patrus suggested that we should put out the kerosine lamp, and go to bed.

'And to bedbugs,' suggested Gangaram.

'Thank God we don't have the mosquitoes,' Patrus added on a more positive note. I snuffed out the lamp.

Waking up with a jerk, I looked around. At first I didn't see anything, but heard a lot of muffled commotion from outside. Then, when my eyes focused in the dark, I noticed the sentry had shut the door. A small amount of light from the electric light bulb outside usually came through the window. However, something was blocking that too. After a while, I saw three heads crowded next to the window. I stood up, and approached my friends.

'Don't make a noise, don't talk,' Patrus whispered softly. 'Just listen and watch.'

I watched, but heard even more. The window faced south; the office door from which the noise came, west. A continuous moaning went on, rather like the whistle of a steam locomotive. Together with this, a sound like that of typing continued.

'Torture, police torture,' Gangaram whispered. 'The victims arrived this evening, remember?'

'What brutes,' Patrus whispered back. 'They take part in it with such relish. One Nepali torturing another.'

Jogbir stood totally mute. I grasped what Patrus meant. I heard the policemen laugh, run back and forth from the office, scold each other for not bringing enough nettles or chilli powder.

For some strange reason, they brought the man onto the grass outside. Policemen stood on both sides. A few watched from behind. The man walked resting both his hands on his knees. Two policemen beat his back, and made him run. The man stumbled. They beat his knees, and again ordered him to run. After about five minutes of this novel game, they took him inside. His wailing moan started a few seconds later.

I lay on my bed, and tried to pray for the victims. I didn't know what they'd done. I noticed the callous, joyful smiles on the policemen's faces as they brought the victim outside. If only I had my machine gun from the war days! I imagined myself shooting the brutes down one by one, going to the victim, grabbing him by his arm, urging him to go home, and running to rescue the man and woman still remaining in the barracks. With the smoking machine gun in hand, I revelled in the few seconds of real Gurkha bravery!

What nonsense! I thought as I shook myself out of my stupor. I turned on my stomach, and prayed that the hands that beat would freeze. I pleaded with *Yesu* to send pity to the hearts of the policemen. I hoped that the victim might not feel pain. I alternated between this heroic imagination and hard reality, the desire for vengeance on the culprits disguised as policemen and the inability to do anything. The victim's moan continued till about two in the morning. In agony the voices of people sound similar, I thought. I guessed they must have tortured the woman some time in between.

We woke up late that morning. Some time later, the constable arrived.

'I've come for my trip to the tea shop,' he said jovially.

I wondered if the constable himself hadn't taken part in the gruesome task scarcely six hours before. 'A lot of noise last night,' I began. 'We got up quite late.'

'Oh, we can sleep through all that,' the constable replied. 'Such things happen regularly in police barracks.'

'What happened?' asked Gangaram innocently.

'Those two men and a woman committed a murder together,' the constable said, 'but no one is confessing it.'

'How did the murder take place?' Gangaram

wanted to get at the story.

'One of the men slept with his daughter-in-law, made her pregnant, and drowned her in a pond. We think the man, his wife, and the man's brother must've killed her.'

'But what if none of them did it?' Patrus asked.

'Who else could've done it? The woman was the most stubborn. The others denied the murder. She didn't even speak. They even shoved nettles into her genitals! Not a word!' The constable realised he'd said too much. He took the money and went for the belated morning tea.

As I stared into the sunlight outside, I saw a decrepit, barefooted man inch slowly along the grass. He had both his palms resting on his knees. He seemed to take a minute to move each foot forward. The low morning sun cast a long shadow on the grass meadow in front of the flag-pole. He moved out of the shade. As soon as all his body bathed in the sunlight, he turned around. I saw the victim's fingers and toes swollen to double their normal size, and beckoned others in the room to have a look. Jogbir went to the window. Patrus and Gangaram stole to the door, and peeped out.

'They must've inserted pins under his finger nails,' Patrus guessed.

'In spite of all the beatings on the knee and the ankle he can still walk, poor man,' I added.

'The police here celebrate Buddha's birthday in a strange way,' Gangaram said. 'What a tribute to Buddha!'

With a thousand horrid thoughts racing in my mind, I kept on gazing at the dejected figure. The victim stopped squatting, and sat with his feet stretched out in the sun. I wondered if the heat deadened the pain.

Wednesday

Well, for most of yesterday I wrote the events of the previous two days. However, I guess the tribute to Buddha wasn't yet enough. The torture continued last night too.

This morning at ten thirty, Sergeant Lal and two constables came to the room we occupied. 'We'll go to court today,' the sergeant said. 'We need one week more for the investigation and so have to apply for permission.'

'Can't you go yourselves? Do we have to come too?' Gangaram asked.

'I'm afraid we all have to go,' the sergeant persisted. 'We must keep the silly rules. The court won't believe we have you in custody unless the officials there see you.'

I dreaded walking through the Trisuli bazaar again. The court lay to the north of the barracks. To reach it, we'd first have to go down to the main cobbled street of the Trisuli bazaar, turn north, and climb up to the small plateau that housed the court. Two policemen, with only batons this time, led the way. Lal and two other constables followed behind. I walked closest to Lal. Jogbir and the two pastors had gone ahead.

'How have we treated you, Mahila *dai?*' the sergeant asked teasingly. I wanted to turn round and slap him on the face, but controlled myself.

'Not bad,' I answered the man I had once bribed. 'When will you send us home?'

'Home? You don't like us then, Mahila *dai?* We have enjoyed having you!'

'Now be serious,' I pleaded. 'You policemen have a knack of playing with others' lives. You do it all in jest. When will you stop harassing us?'

'We'll probably take you to your village tomorrow morning. If all the people say you haven't done anything wrong, you can remain there.'

'We've told you we worship *Yesu,* can't you decide from that? Why do you need the whole village to witness to what we've freely admitted?'

'We have to follow certain legal procedures, we can't do what we like,' the sergeant responded. We reached the cobblestones of the bazaar.

I looked around for anyone from Dhanee Gaon. I saw Ratan in a shop far away. Fortunately, he didn't turn around, and thus spared me the agony of blushing. The rest who watched me were townsfolk whom I didn't mind.

The path turned north and uphill towards the court. I saw the colours of Nepal fluttering on a water pipe – the improvised flag-pole. As a proud soldier, I had saluted the flag many times each day. Now it appeared to me more like the fangs of the oppressor. A few urchins raced ahead of the group to the courtyard where the flag-pole stood. As the policemen approached them, they said something nasty and ran away. I couldn't tell whether the urchins were cursing us or the policemen.

We didn't even enter the court building. While we sat on the grass in the excessive heat of the sun, Lal went in with his files; and the two constables followed. A man grabbed Lal by his arm and joked about something. I had seen him sitting next to the prosecutor on Buddha's birthday. Then I heard the man remarking to the sergeant how he'd never dealt with a case involving Christians. After disappearing for a few minutes, the sergeant walked out of the court door.

'All finished,' the sergeant told Gangaram. 'Now we can deliver you to the court within the next seven days. One more week of our hospitality.'

'We may weep when we leave you,' said Gangaram pungently. The sergeant smiled. I felt refreshed after the walk to the court. The silly rules were not without their advantages!

Refreshment turned to gloom back at the barracks when a short chap came up railing at

Jogbir. 'You convict!' the fellow screamed. 'Why have you dirtied the inspector's toilet? Go and clean it, go immediately!' The person stood red and gesticulating in front of Jogbir. I'd seen Jogbir go behind the house, but I could hardly believe my friend had used the officer's toilet!

'I didn't do it,' Jogbir replied. 'Don't call me a convict either!'

'You did, liar! I'll blast your teeth out.' The authority the simple toilet sweeper claimed totally baffled us. I saw Gangaram stand up.

'I'll clean it,' Gangaram said. 'We don't mind getting our hands dirty.' Subdued a bit, the toilet sweeper led Gangaram to the site. A few minutes later, Gangaram came away with a peculiar smile. Meanwhile, the sentry approached them.

'That rascal! They found him too short for a constable, and made him an orderly to the inspector instead,' the sentry said. 'Because he serves the inspector, he thinks he can scold anyone. The inspector's children dirty the toilet a hundred times a day,' the sentry added. 'Probably that has caused the fellow's frustration.'

When the gong struck two, we decided to have tea in the privacy of our room. Sergeant Lal came and announced that we'd have to get ready at six tomorrow to walk to Dhanee Gaon. Our destiny now lies in the hands of the villagers. If the villagers testify a hundred per cent on our behalf, we may not even return to the barracks tomorrow. Whatever the outcome, I look forward to the walk. Strangely, I've begun to appreciate the physical training I loathed during my military days. However, I felt puzzled at the orders the sergeant gave us. If we are to leave that early tomorrow, will we get the rice meal which we usually have at ten?

Half an hour later, Sergeant Lal came again, this time with a file of papers. 'Jogbir Tamang,' he called. Jogbir stood up. 'You should take your belongings and go home,' Lal addressed him cheerfully, as if to make up for the ordeal Jogbir had gone through a few hours before.

'Go home, alone?'

'Yes, we said if you gave the correct answers you'd all go free. So far, only Jogbir has done so.'

'What did I say?' Jogbir gazed at the sergeant in astonishment.

'All the others said they worship *Yesu*.' The sergeant turned to a paper in his file and pointed to a line. 'You said in your report that you worship the God of Abraham, Isaac and Jacob. The prosecutor has asked us to let you go.'

'But I still follow *Yesu*,' protested Jogbir.

'If the sergeant sahib tells you to go free, you should obey,' Patrus suggested and winked.

'All right, I'll go,' Jogbir replied sadly. The sergeant left. Renu, Jogbir's taking an extremely long time to pack up. He doesn't want to leave us. He's discussing different things with both the pastors. His delay has given me the time to bring you up to date. He should give you the rest of our news. We'll meet tomorrow.

Father

CHAPTER
EIGHT

THE VISITS

Perhaps Renu should not have read Father's letter late into the previous night. She could not fall asleep thinking of the people who had been tortured. Her imagination played tricks with her, and she heard their screams as if they were undergoing the ordeal next door. When day broke, her eyes were red like tomatoes. Walking to church with Mother, she explained the gist of what she had read. Mother started sobbing right on the path thinking what would happen to her husband. Renu reminded her of the presence of the two pastors with him, and comforted her. It was a while before Sanumaya regained her composure, and continued the trip towards the church. They noticed a huge crowd outside. The people spilled over to the courtyard of Patrus' house next door. Renu saw faces never seen before.

People gather to see the bad as well as the good! she thought.

She resented the fact that her father provided part of the amusement. Some people remarked about his previous drinking bouts. Most of them had come to see the horses the sub-inspector and the sergeant rode. The two had arrived quite early, tethered their animals, and gone off for a stroll.

At last Renu and Sanumaya saw the prisoners and the police slowly climb up the slope. A murmur swept over the crowd. Renu kept on gazing at her father who walked roughly in the middle of the line. She could hardly believe he had experienced the trials he wrote about. He seemed delighted to be back in his village.

As soon as the contingent arrived at the courtyard, Renu saw Patrus go to the verandah of his house, and slump down. She ran to Father who stroked her hair. Renu's eyes watered as Sanumaya drew near.

'I haven't done anything wrong,' Mahila consoled her. 'The Lord will protect me.'

'We've visited the *Pradhan Panch* many times already,' Sanumaya plucked up courage to speak. 'We'll keep on pushing him till he gets you out. Do you know the police tricked him, and arrested all of you?'

'I didn't,' Mahila replied, ' but I know they'll do anything for a few extra rupees.'

Renu saw Esther and Jogbir emerge through the door. Esther walked to her husband.

'Welcome back, stranger!' she exclaimed.

'See, I've become a stranger already,' Patrus remarked to Gangaram. 'I want to lie on this verandah to take away some of home with me.'

'You miss home badly, I'm sure.' Esther patted her husband on the back. 'Come in for lunch. That'll make you even more homesick.' Sushila came to say she had the table all ready.

Mahila walked over to Jogbir. 'Hello, free man!' Mahila teased him.

'Please don't,' Jogbir replied. 'I'd rather sleep next to you in that dingy room than lead the service here this Saturday. *Pastorni ama* has already given me that job.'

'How I'd like to change places with you!' Mahila followed the two pastors into the dining room. Renu took her place in the kitchen with Esther and Sushila.

'The police have refused to come,' Esther said. 'We'll have to start. I've sent Sudeep to call them twice already.'

'They'll eat,' replied Patrus. 'We'll wait a while.'

After the three sat down at the table, Sudeep walked out as if he had forgotten something. A few minutes later he emerged with a camera.

'I'll have to take pictures,' Sudeep said. 'Things like this don't happen in Darjeeling.' 'Careful,' warned his father. 'The police and the military are not too keen on cameras!' Sudeep nodded and disappeared.

After her father and the pastors had eaten, Renu followed the group outside. She observed a long line of people waiting at the door of the church. She scrutinized the faces, and wondered who would testify against her father and who would take his side. 'When I come out, I'll send you to school,'

Mahila said softly. 'I want my daughter to train as a nurse.'

'Please don't speak any more about that now,' Renu advised. 'People may hear of it and laugh. Come home first.'

'I wanted to say at least that much,' Mahila said, 'so that you may have hope for the future. I'll save every rupee from the pension I get. I'll see you through.'

'All right, Father, all right,' Renu replied. 'Come home first.'

Sanumaya listened quietly to the ambitions of both her husband and daughter. Soon, Renu observed that the line had begun to move. Gangaram and Patrus sat on the verandah opposite her. Mahila left her to join them.

'I thought the hearing of witnesses would take place only in our presence. They've begun already,' Gangaram remarked. Renu sat attentive.

'I don't care,' Patrus replied. 'They're just putting on an entertainment for the villagers.'

'You should care,' Gangaram replied. 'Do you want to spend six years in jail?'

Just then Jogbir appeared.

'The sub-inspector scolds anyone who speaks for us. He encourages our opponents to babble on. We should complain,' Jogbir looked distressed.

'I won't,' Patrus replied. 'In the end God will judge. I want to lie down here.'

'If you won't, I will,' Gangaram retorted. He got up and walked into the church with Jogbir.

'The prosecutor's come out,' Renu heard Father say. Gangaram and Jogbir took him to one side. Gangaram gesticulated his complaints. The prosecutor nodded his head, and approached Patrus.

'Sir,' he said. 'For the peace of all, you also should go in. The villagers should testify only in your presence.'

'Let's go in and hear stories about us,' Mahila shouted to Renu. Shy at the suggestion, she looked at her mother. Sanumaya nodded. Renu followed Mahila into the church hall, but took her seat behind the prisoners along with other inquisitive villagers. Mahila went to the front to sit alongside the two pastors. Opposite him sat the sergeant, the prosecutor, the sub-inspector, and the *Pradhan Panch*. Renu saw Father's eyes meet those of his distant uncle. The latter looked down. She felt pity for the king of the village. Obviously, the policemen were playing games with him too.

'This whole thing's a facade,' Gangaram said softly to Patrus. 'These villagers haven't even seen the baptism we took part in. Yet they're witnessing to fantastic things about us, and the sergeant is writing everything down.'

'Precisely so,' replied Patrus. 'No wonder I couldn't care less.' The Christians heard and wondered at the testimonies:

'These men eat beef and teach us to do the same.'

'They've corrupted the entire village.'

'The gods haven't sent rain because of them.'

'They don't shave their heads at funerals.'

'They've slaughtered cows.'

'They pollute our water taps.'

'The *lamas* in the village will soon lose their jobs.'

'They don't marry our sons or daughters.'

'The leader comes from Darjeeling. We should expel him.'

'The people of Dhanee Gaon certainly have imagination,' Gangaram whispered to Patrus after about an hour.

'That's why I couldn't care less,' Patrus repeated his indifference.

Renu saw Sudeep slowly enter through the door. The sub-inspector had his ears tuned to the testimony of an old man, and did not notice the budding photographer. Sudeep aimed the camera at the officers, and clicked.

'Get the camera, get it!' the sub-inspector shouted at the constables outside. Mahila saw Patrus turn pale. Sudeep ran through the door.

'What a foolish boy,' Patrus moaned, 'I warned him so many times.'

'Perhaps they won't catch him,' muttered Gangaram.

The testifying took almost three hours. Everyone who spoke had to sign to what had just been uttered. At last, the prisoners gave their signatures admitting that the procedure had been completed in their presence. After Mahila scrawled his, Renu followed him to the verandah of Patrus' house. She again heard the familiar remarks: how the whole thing had been a facade, how the destiny of the prisoners had already been determined, how hopeless the situation appeared. Father patted Renu on the head, and whispered that he would continue writing even though he did not know how to get the letters out to her. Then, as if choking on something, Mahila stood speechless for a while.

'In spite of all this, Renu,' her father remarked at last, 'the visit was worth it!'

***

Without having her morning rice, Renu went to church that Saturday. She had just drunk a cup of tea with her mother. Sanumaya joined her in fasting just to miss the cooking for half a day. Jogbir had announced that those who could should come on an empty stomach. The service would focus on praying about the events that had just occurred. Renu believed Esther had given him the idea of the prayer meeting.

Jogbir can never replace our pastor, Renu thought as she heard the substitute ramble on. He missed out the offertory hymn altogether, and scratched his head often because he could not find the Bible verses he wanted. Of course, he could not lead the songs, and so Sudeep started most of the hymns on his guitar while Shankar played his *madal*. Yet Renu still felt the deep presence of God. A great cloud of love seemed to envelope her. Her heart warmed in a strange way. After some time, Jogbir announced that the children could go to Sunday school.

Wanting to avoid the fuss of other Christians over her father, Renu skipped the prayers and went to Sunday school. She appreciated the concern, but felt awkward nevertheless.

Looking behind, Renu saw Sudeep hurry after her to Thuli's home. Soon he caught up with her. 'I know how you feel,' Sudeep said awkwardly, 'but we're suffering with you. We belong to this great worldwide family. God found fit to keep my father with yours.'

'He did,' Renu answered feebly.

'I'll go to Darjeeling soon.' Sudeep changed the subject. 'Would you like to come with me? I have to take the news to my family first hand. My father doesn't want all sorts of rumour reaching them. Would you like to see Darjeeling?'

Renu blushed, and did not know what to reply. Just then Sushila arrived with the other children.

Renu saw Thuli come out of the door to see if she had put the straw mats on the verandah. Thuli looked depressed and sullen. Rumour had it that her husband Karna had gone somewhere else on business. Tamangs usually did not keep secrets, and among the Christians everyone knew what the others were doing. Where had Karna gone so quietly? That day Thuli did not want to sit and listen. She left them and went inside.

When Sunday school ended, Renu went back to church. Jogbir was still relating the account of the arrest. Prayers had not begun after all! He mentioned the heroism of Gangaram and Patrus in refusing freedom. He described the food they received, and attributed it only to the presence of the educated pastors whom the police respected. He also stated the tortures the three victims underwent, and asked the congregation to pray for them.

'Above all we should pray for the king and queen of the country,' Jogbir suggested. 'They can change these unjust laws overnight if God leads them to.' He went on to explain what the police really wanted.

'The constable who bought our morning tea once said we would all go free if we offered a thousand rupees each. Of course, our conscience wouldn't allow us to do such a thing.' The congregation looked intently at Jogbir.

'The authorities are out to rob us. In other areas, the police have feasted on chickens belonging to Christians; and then, at the end of the day, arrested them!'

Renu had heard enough, and longed for real prayer to start. After rambling on for half an hour more, Jogbir finally stopped.

The Christians put their heads to the straw mats. In the beginning all prayed aloud together. When the noisy supplication subsided, different people led in prayer; and others responded with 'amen'. Renu noted that most of the prayers concentrated on the two pastors, but her father did get an occasional mention.

The prayer meeting would continue the whole day. In the late afternoon, Renu decided to go home. She needed to comfort her mother who recently had begun to dread being alone. As Renu took to the path, an idea which had come to her during the prayer meeting, returned to her.

'We should go and visit Father,' Sanumaya suggested to Renu as soon as she entered the house. 'The police may have more sympathy for him when they see us, two poor women.'

'I thought the same too,' agreed Renu.

'When will we go?'

'Tomorrow,' replied her daughter.

'Tomorrow?' asked Sanumaya. 'Well, why not? I need to do some shopping as well. Father always did it before. Now I appreciate how much he helped me. We don't have enough oil and salt for another day. The shop on top of Tarachuli always charges more.'

'Well, it has to get everything from Trisuli,' Renu reminded her.

'I'd rather go to Trisuli bazaar myself. We'll visit Father first, and then you can return home early to water the cattle. I'll come after the shopping.'

'I'd better wash my blouse and *fariah*,' Renu said. 'Shall I wash yours too? The *Baisakh* heat will dry them through the night.' Sanumaya searched for her clothes, and gave them to her daughter. Renu meditated on what they'd say to Father the next day, and felt excited. She noticed her mother cheer up too.

***

Exactly one week before, Renu's father had followed the path which she and her mother now took. Renu did not like walking behind her mother. The thongs her mother wore gave out a small cloud of yellow dust. Renu decided to get closer, but thought it improper to get ahead of her.

They agreed not to have tea at the foot of the hill. Renu knew her father never went on without it; but he also chatted with the shopkeeper who, seeing the ladies walking, offered them free cups of tea.

'We've just had our rice,' Sanumaya replied, and the two hurried on.

Along the way, Sanumaya advised her daughter, 'I've decided never to accept free gifts. You make enemies easily that way. Why put yourself under obligation to anyone?'

'I'm sure you're right,' Renu said. 'You've lived more than

I have!'

'Hard lessons through many tears,' Sanumaya assured her daughter. 'You take a free cup of tea, and later on the person may oblige you to do something. You can hardly say "no" then.' In the distance, Renu saw a man approach them. He had a black umbrella over his head.

'I should have brought my umbrella,' said Sanumaya regretfully. 'I didn't need it coming down, but going up will kill me. The *Baisakh* sun can do a lot of harm!'

'I haven't got one, so I didn't even think of it,' Renu replied.

'The cloth on mine looks so tattered that I was ashamed to bring it. I'm walking with dignity now,' Sanumaya joked, 'but I'll suffer going up.'

'Start your journey after the sun goes down a bit,' Renu advised. 'You'll find it much easier then.'

The man with the umbrella drew closer. 'That looks like the pastor's son, Sudeep,' noted Renu. Sanumaya gazed at the figure more intently.

'Of course,' Sanumaya replied. 'I wonder if he's been to visit Father. We should ask him.'

Sudeep drew closer, smiled, and greeted the women with a *namasthe*.

'Sudeep *babu*, we must sit down and talk somewhere. Did you meet your father?'

'I did,' Sudeep replied. 'They have more company now!'

'You mean they arrested more?' Sanumaya gasped as she led Sudeep to the shade under a tree.

'Yes, one is called Bharat, the other Sam. They came to visit Pastor Gangaram on the day the police brought him, Renu's father, and my father to our village. The *CDO* arrested them too.'

'*Ram, Ram*,' Sanumaya gasped. Renu looked annoyed because the Christians did not call on that deity. Sudeep smiled.

'Are you going to visit Renu's father today?' Sudeep asked.

'Just for a while. After that I have to do shopping. Renu will return home early. The cattle will need water and fodder.'

'Well,' replied Sudeep. 'I'd better go now.' Sudeep pressed a button on the umbrella he had already folded. It spread out in style. Soon, Renu saw only the umbrella and a pair of legs walking away in the opposite direction.

Renu observed her mother in a meditative mood.

'I smelled a strange odour,' Sanumaya remarked. 'The boy must have had a drink to cheer himself up.'

'I don't believe it,' Renu replied. 'Christians don't drink!'

'He smelled just like your father a few months ago!'

'Incredible,' Renu answered. 'All these problems have affected your senses too!'

'I swear by *Ram*,' Sanumaya insisted.

'Even then I don't believe you.' Renu sounded irritated.

'Oh well, don't let's argue any more,' responded Sanumaya wearily.

***

The sentry called Mahila. The two pastors peeped out of the door. Renu and Sanumaya instinctively folded their hands in greeting.

'Let's sit under the banyan tree,' Mahila suggested. 'We usually go there, but today we've decided to have a day of fasting and prayer.'

'We had the same in our church yesterday,' Renu replied.

'Yes, I know. Last Thursday Jogbir told me that he'd call for serious prayer,' said Mahila beckoning his wife and daughter to sit on the stone stool around the tree. 'God can free us if He wants to.'

'If He wants?' Renu replied. 'Don't talk like that.'

'Well, I fear the Bible links the call of God and suffering very closely. I was reading how God called Paul for His service. Acts chapter 9, verse 15 mentions Paul's call; the next verse, the suffering Paul must undergo. Go home and read them, Renu. Those two verses blessed me a lot.'

'Father, who suggested you should fast and pray?'

'I did, Renu, I did. You don't know how much the whole event has weighed on me. Pastor Gangaram came from Kathmandu for my baptism. Our pastor took the step because I asked for it. Now, because of me they also suffer. I wanted to fast and pray alone, but they joined in. Then the police caused problems.'

'What happened?' Renu asked.

'This morning when we asked the cook not to prepare anything for us, the sub-inspector himself came to the room. He pleaded with us not to go on a hunger strike!'

'Hunger strike?'

'Yes, that happens when prisoners fast until they get what they want or die. We assured him that we'd eat in the evening. That alone put his mind at rest. Even then, some other policemen came to persuade us to eat. Hindus fast; they couldn't understand Christians fasting and praying.'

'Did you pray for anything particular this morning?' Sanumaya broke in for the first time.

'You won't understand, but I prayed that *Yesu*'s will may prevail in my life,' Mahila replied looking intently at his wife.

'Pray that He'll free you fast. We need you back home,' Sanumaya pleaded fervently. Renu saw her father smile a bit.

'I miss your cooking too,' Mahila looked at his wife. 'I didn't realise how much care you put into it. Even *dhindo* tasted much better from your hands.' Mahila winked and pulled at Renu's cheek gently. 'She grows more beautiful each day, doesn't she?' he said.

'She'll seem even more pretty when you come home.' Mahila saw the two pastors making signs at him from the door.

'I have to go now, but don't worry about me. Things look better,' Mahila assured them.

'How?'

'Yesterday the accountant of the barracks came to talk with us. He'd drunk a lot, and told us things he should've kept quiet about. He admitted, for example, that he had stolen twenty-six thousand rupees by putting in bogus expenses... Anyway, he said that once the police deliver us to the court, we can bail ourselves out, and fight the case from home. It costs nearly four thousand rupees for each person. Pastors Gangaram and Patrus both vow to bail me out.'

'May God bless them,' sighed Renu.

'Finally, tell me, is the cow still giving milk?' Mahila changed the subject.

'It is, but only about two glasses a day, just enough for tea,' Sanumaya brought her husband up to date. 'It may stop in a month's time.'

'But two months later the buffalo may give birth?' Mahila

remembered.

'Yes, it will.'

'Not bad,' Mahila said. 'You can manage a month without milk, can't you?'

Mahila saw Patrus making signs at him again.

'If I talk too much, they may not allow you to visit me again. My pastor spoke for only five minutes to his son this morning. I'd better go. Don't worry.' Renu saw Father glance at them from the door of his room, and smile faintly. The pastors peeped out, and waved at her and Sanumaya.

After Mother went off towards Trisuli bazaar, Renu clutched at the five rupees she had received, and panted along as fast as she could. Mother urged her at least to have tea from the shop at the foot of the hill. Instead, she drank plenty of water at the tap next to the barrage. When Renu got to the shop, she found the shopkeeper bending over and blowing at the fire-place. She felt relieved, and walked hurriedly up the path till she could see the shop no more.

What would people think if they saw me drinking tea alone with the shopkeeper? She asked herself and slowed her pace. She knew a spring an hour's climb up. She would drink more water there. She saw the banyan tree that must have given shade to her ancestors countless times. As she was very tired by now, she determined to sit there, and rest a while. She put the five-rupee note into the tip of her *fariah*, and tied it in with a small knot.

When she approached the banyan tree, she saw someone sitting on the stone slab. He was facing the opposite direction, so Renu just saw his back.

'Oh,' Renu fumbled, as Sudeep turned around and smiled at her. 'I thought you must have reached home long ago!'

'I can't walk as fast as you,' Sudeep replied. 'I have to rest every now and then. Come and sit down for a few minutes.'

'No, I shan't,' Renu said, wiping her sweaty face with the sleeves of her blouse. 'The cattle must have died of thirst by now.'

'Then I'll come too!' Sudeep followed her.

Renu prayed silently that no one she knew would go to Trisuli at that hour. She dreaded the rumours that would circulate in the village if anyone saw her with Sudeep. He had

123

deliberately waited for her! All because of Mother, thought Renu. She had to blabber out that I'd return early!

Renu did not respond to many of the things that Sudeep said. He mentioned he would leave Trisuli for Kathmandu on Tuesday at noon, and would take the night bus to Darjeeling the same evening. Patrus wanted him to visit Gangaram's family, and reassure his own relatives back in Darjeeling. Would Renu like to go with him? He asked again. Renu saw a man and a woman heading downhill towards them. Fortunately, they did not know her.

Realising the full implication of what Sudeep had suggested, Renu felt her heart beat faster. For the first time in her life, a lad had fallen in love with her!

'Turn around,' she heard Sudeep call. Click! Renu blushed as she saw the camera.

'I almost had to cry in front of the sub-inspector to get it back,' Sudeep admitted. 'He asked me to hand over the film inside. I bought another one in Trisuli. It costs a lot more here.'

Renu did not respond. Neither did her heart stop racing. They came to the fork that separated the church from Renu's home.

'Think about it,' Sudeep urged. 'I'll take the noon bus on Tuesday.'

Renu noticed Sudeep glance at her several times from the separate path he took. Twice their eyes met. Renu blushed and smiled. Sudeep looked radiant.

What a day, Renu sighed to herself. I should have walked back with Mother!

Finally, Sudeep vanished out of her sight.

Had Renu returned home with Mother, the cattle would have died! The animals quickly got through the two vessels of water in the house. Renu ran to the tap to fetch more. After doing three trips back and forth, she stroked the bulging side of the pregnant buffalo; and wondered whether a male or a female calf lay inside. The calf looked at her jealously. She went over, and stroked its head too.

Renu had already lit her lamp when Mother arrived. She rushed to lift the heavy bag off her shoulder. Sanumaya noticed Renu had cleaned the spinach for the curry.

'You cook today,' she requested. 'I know how tired you

must feel, but you've not seen the years I have. Besides, you didn't have to carry the bag!'

Renu did not protest. She took out what Mother had bought. She marvelled at her thrift. Renu stored away the salt which would last them another three months, and the bottle of oil which would not stretch that far. She had bought nothing else. Renu also marvelled at Mother's generosity. She had never given her a five-rupee note before. She urged Mother to go up and rest.

Mother did not rest. 'I've thought of something,' Sanumaya said.

'What?'

'We should have left some money with Father today. Good ideas come to my head too late. Perhaps Father could give a bit to the accountant or even to the head officer when he next visits the room.'

'Perhaps he could,' Renu replied.

'Renu, at my age I don't look forward to walking. Why don't you go tomorrow, and meet Father again? Give him some money. I think you should take at least two hundred rupees.'

'I need rest too,' Renu frowned back.

'Then go on Tuesday,' Sanumaya suggested. Her daughter nodded in agreement.

'Two hundred rupees! Can you manage with so little in the house?'

'I can, somehow,' Mother replied. 'The money may help Father. If he can't use it, he'll save it.'

'But the pastors have agreed to bail him out; does he really need it?'

'Yes,' replied Sanumaya.' If possible, I'd like to do without their help too.'

Has prayer and fasting softened Mother? Renu wondered, looking forward to another visit with Father.

CHAPTER NINE

DARJEELING

That Tuesday morning, Renu thought she was walking the dusty path downhill for the last time in her life. She did not know if she would ever return to Dhanee Gaon. She had not slept much during the night for thinking of the course of action she would take. She clutched at the shoulder bag resting at her side and felt the purse. She had never gone on a long journey before, and did not know what to carry. Her cloth purse, the *fariah* and the blouse she had worn the Sunday before, and her New Testament, which Sushila had presented to her after Mother had torn the old one, filled her bag. She determined to buy a proper lady's bag as soon as she reached Kathmandu. She felt the money her purse contained: two hundred rupees Mother had given for her father, and the five rupees which she had saved.

I'll break Mother's heart, she thought, but I have to do it!

Mother had noted how pretty she looked in her blue blouse and the matching blue sari, the only one she had. To her relief, Mother did not say anything more. As she walked along briskly, she decided she had made the correct move.

Her prospects for education in the village remained bleak. Father could change his mind once he got out. Sudeep had mentioned how many different schools Darjeeling had. He had promised to educate her. He did not know her desire to train as a nurse, but she would tell him that on the bus.

Her prospects for marriage in Dhanee Gaon looked even bleaker. She could think of no one close to her age but Shankar, and she did not like him. She had heard of some Christian girls in Kathmandu eloping with Hindu men, and both the societies detested them. Renu envisaged the problem getting less severe in another generation, but not in her own. Christian

Tamangs from Lama Gahra or even Kathmandu may ask for her hand, but if so why not from Darjeeling?

Besides admiring Sudeep's musical abilities, Renu thought he had a kind heart as well. She could not forget how he tried to comfort her when the news of the arrest first came. Sudeep had assured her of baptism once they reached Darjeeling. Then, the wedding would follow. In Sudeep she found the means to banish the drudgery of the village life and the future uncertainties for ever.

If she had stabbed her parents in the back, they deserved it. They had deprived her of education. Besides, after the dust settled, she would write to them. She thought she would be more useful as a trained nurse. She could even take her parents to Darjeeling to live out their old age. Renu's eyes sparkled as she imagined her parents blessing her for all the help Sudeep and she would offer.

Renu tried not to look at the tea shop. When the shopkeeper noticed her, she dreaded he would invite her for the usual free cup of tea. Instead, he grinned at her, and did not utter a word. She pretended to be in a hurry.

Renu paused for a while at the fork that led either up to the police barracks or down to the bazaar and the bus station. She felt something eat away at her as she walked downhill. She went to a shop, and asked what time it was. Eleven fifteen. Renu sighed in relief.

Perhaps Sudeep will arrive within half an hour, she thought, and sat lightly on a stone in the shade. People had begun loading the roof-rack of the bus.

Besides the suitcases and the trunks, the roof had baskets of live chickens and two goats which bleated away nervously from their elevated position. One urinated, and the coolie below cursed it for spraying his hair. Renu smiled. People of all sorts and two western hippies crowded about the ticket man seated near the bus. They argued about seats in the back and front. Renu heard one man pleading for one next to the window because he usually vomited during the trip. More luggage and three roosters in narrow bamboo baskets went to the roof. To Renu's surprise, the hippies gladly climbed up too.

Simultaneously, Renu pitied the chickens and worried about Sudeep. If he did not arrive in time, they would have to wait till the next morning. Who knows who might see them together, and take the report to her parents? The minutes ticked away on the grandfather clock in the shop. Each 'tick' made Renu more anxious.

At last he was coming! In the distance Renu saw Sudeep walking with a medium-sized brown suitcase. He appeared to be on the lookout for Renu. Eventually, he noticed her outside the shop. Sudeep waved his hand and approached her.

Placing the suitcase next to Renu, Sudeep took his wallet out. 'I'll leave this here; I'll have to get the tickets!' he said. Renu watched Sudeep gesticulating with the ticket man who moved his head from side to side in extreme irritation. She felt something had gone wrong. Then she saw Sudeep take money out of the wallet.

'I couldn't get a seat in the front,' Sudeep explained on his return. 'The man offered me the seat next to the door because no one likes to sit there. Well, I do!' Sudeep put the wallet back in his pocket, and patted it.

When the bus finally started moving, Renu turned back, and looked at the hill that sheltered her village. Would she ever return? Thus far she did not recognise anyone in the bus. She guessed no one from her village sat in it, and felt more comfortable. She started feeling more comfortable next to Sudeep too. The narrow seat did not offer much room for both of them. She pressed herself as much to the window as she could.

Three hours later, Renu had her first view of Kathmandu. She noticed the electric wires that zigzagged Balaju, the wide circular road which went around the capital, the cemented houses, and the numerous cars. She had her eyes glued on the window, and forgot Sudeep was sitting next to her.

'We have to get out in a few minutes,' Sudeep said, 'I'd better tell you of our plans. We'll go to the night-bus station. There you'll stay with the luggage while I rush quickly to Pastor Gangaram's home.'

'I want to buy a bag,' Renu replied, 'a lady's bag.'

'We'll do that too,' Sudeep assured her.

Sudeep hired a taxi, and explained the sights they saw along the way: the science college, Hotel Malla where only rich people and foreigners had the means to stay, the royal palace on the left, the clock tower, and Ratna Park. Finally, the taxi ground to a halt. During the rainy season, the bus station would have fitted Patrus' description she had heard the previous year at school. It lay in a dip, and clouds of dust arose as each vehicle entered or left the area. Her first experience of the capital city did not look promising.

Four or five dirtily dressed lads approached Sudeep as he pulled his suitcase out of the taxi and paid the driver. Renu noticed that each wanted them to get tickets for the bus company he worked for. Sudeep looked beyond them to a table in front of rooms at the western edge of the station.

'Let's go,' he said to Renu. 'We'll have to choose a bus company that has a room for you to wait in.'

The man at the table looked at Sudeep in expectation.

'Do you have a waiting room? This lady's to remain there till I finish some business.'

'Just behind me,' the ticket seller assured him. 'You'll find other people there too.'

'I'll come for the tickets,' said Sudeep and guided Renu into the room. Putting down the luggage next to a bench, Sudeep took out his wallet again, and walked to the table. Renu watched the men, women, and children packed on the four benches, and wondered where all the people could be travelling to. Sudeep returned with two pieces of paper in his hand.

'Here, keep these in your bag. I'll take a taxi, and come back soon. We have only two hours before the bus leaves.'

Renu marvelled at how busy her fiancé looked. He impressed her with his knack of organising things. Expecting him to return in a jiffy, she eagerly looked forward to taking a walk with him towards the shops nearby to purchase a bag. She looked around enviously at the ladies in the room. None of them had anything like her pitiful shoulder bag. In a shop with Sudeep, she imagined herself fussing at the items she saw.

As she stared through the door, one bus after another left. She wondered which bus she was to take, whether Sudeep would return in time at all. Not having a watch, she asked the lady sitting next to her how late it was getting.

'Half past five,' she said. ' Don't worry; show me your tickets.'

Renu was afraid to give her both the tickets, and showed her one.

'It says six on top, you see. We'll be on the same bus. Your husband will know!'

Renu blushed at the mention of 'husband', but she did not make the effort to explain matters.

How could the woman know? She kept asking herself this question. More buses left.

Renu's anxiety ended when she spotted Sudeep at the door. Carrying a wrapped package in his hand, he handed it over to Renu. 'For you,' said Sudeep, 'something you've always wanted.' Like a child, Renu opened the package.

'Oh, how beautiful!' she exclaimed and pulled out a shiny leather bag. The lady next to her noted her joy.

'Wonderful! I wish I had a husband who loved me so much,' she said. Then ominously she added, 'Men get tired of their wives very quickly!'

Renu blushed again, but kept quiet as before. She emptied the contents of her old bag into the newly received gift. Then she neatly folded the cloth bag and pushed that in too.

'Most people throw away the old one as soon as they get a new one. You've kept both!' the lady remarked.

'My father bought it for me,' Renu replied. 'I can hardly throw it away now. Maybe, after a few days.' In a few seconds Renu followed Sudeep out and into the bus.

'On this bus we have separate seats to ourselves,' Sudeep said, 'and the seat goes down like this when you want to sleep.' Sudeep showed Renu how to press the lever and make the seat recline.

'Wonderful,' answered Renu, 'but I won't sleep. I want to watch the scenery the whole night.'

'After a few hours you'll watch nothing but darkness,' Sudeep explained. 'We should rest as much as we can. We shan't reach Darjeeling until four tomorrow evening. I don't want you to look too tired.'

After the bus began to move, Sudeep started to talk. He told Renu how he had warned Pastor Gangaram's wife not to send anyone to the police barracks again.

'The person who'll go next may have twenty thousand rupees with him for bail. He'd better not end up like the last two!'

'But how will the pastors get the money to the court then?'

'The fellow should try going to Dhanee Gaon first. It means more walking, but at least no more arrests. From there, Jogbir could take the money to the court.'

Renu felt happy at Sudeep's advice to Gangaram's wife. If all went well, Father would return home within a week. She prided herself in the role her fiancé had played in gaining his freedom. The bus began to shake and jerk in a strange rhythm that would continue the whole night.

Renu meditated on all the things Sudeep had said. When he talked, he did it with abandon. He revealed that he had failed three times and not passed high school after all! She did not feel too bad about this. Perhaps she and Sudeep could study together. Originally, looking for a job, he had come not to Dhanee Gaon, but to Kathmandu. Only despair had driven him to Dhanee Gaon. He confessed he did not like his father doing the job of a pastor.

A while after the conversation ended, Renu found Sudeep dozing off. She tried to concentrate on the positive things he had said. She did not find many. She tried to remember the good things he did. The pretty bag he bought for her stood out.

I've chosen him for better or worse, thought Renu. She determined to set him straight. Didn't someone say to her that most men improve after marriage? Would he give heed to her attempts at reform? Had she not cheapened herself by eloping with him? Had he previously asked other girls to run away with him? Had they refused? Renu looked lovingly at him, and tried hard to suppress the negative thoughts.

Renu felt fortunate to have the window next to her. Having had little sleep the night before, she felt her stomach churn within her. She wanted to open the window and vomit. However, she feared Sudeep might discover it and the jungly village girl she tried to hide in herself. She put her head down, and waited as long as she could.

I can't hold it any longer, she said to herself and slid open the window pane. In the next moment, the last remnant of the morning rice left her stomach. She slid the window back quickly, and stole a glance at Sudeep. In spite of the fresh gust of wind through the window, he still lay fast asleep.

Thank you *Yesu*, Renu said to herself in relief.

She needed something to wipe her mouth. After using the inner lining of the shoulder bag, she planned to rinse her mouth at the first water spout when the bus stopped next.

The noise of people walking awoke Renu. She did not know when she too had dozed off!

'Mugling! Have your food here,' the bus conductor shouted. 'No other stops! Have your food here!'

Sudeep woke up, looked at his watch, and then gazed at Renu.

'You're hungry,' Sudeep said.

'No I'm not really,' Renu replied, parting her lips as little as possible.

'Then I'll go out and have something.' Sudeep stood up and filed out with the line of people leaving the bus. Renu pretended to go back to sleep, but out of the corner of her eye she noted which restaurant Sudeep entered. After he had vanished between the rows of chairs, tables, and the people eating at them, Renu emerged from the bus. She had spotted a tap in front of the restaurant.

Going to it, she rinsed her mouth and gargled. Two, three, four times! Satisfied, she returned to the vehicle.

I'll not vomit again, she thought, no more food till I get to Darjeeling!

She need not have worried about her smelly mouth. The whole bus reeked with cigarette smoke after the people boarded it again. The bus had NO SMOKING notices in different places, but that did not make any difference. Satisfied by the meal he had just enjoyed, the driver started playing Hindi music over the loudspeakers. Renu noticed Sudeep enter, tottering a bit. Renu kept her eyes shut.

'Still sleeping,' Sudeep murmured.

In a few minutes, Sudeep had dozed off again. Renu smelled something peculiar. She nudged closer to Sudeep. His breath, she said to herself, his breath! Where had she come across that smell? Evil memories swept through her mind. Her father lay dead drunk, holding a piece of firewood in his hand! Mahila struggled as she tried to wrench it away from him by force. He cursed her. The pungent smell wounded her as she finally pulled it away. *Yesu*, Renu whispered, drunk! Renu kept as close to the window as she could. The smell tortured her.

133

As most drunkards do, Sudeep slept soundly. As long as she remained awake, Renu tried to think of plans to get Sudeep away from the bottle. She wondered how he had managed to hide the habit from his parents and other Christians in Dhanee Gaon. Her mother had been right after all – Sudeep had been drinking the previous Sunday! For a while she tried to pray. *Yesu* seemed so far away. A strange sort of loneliness gripped her. Then she dozed off.

The sun rises faster in the plains, she thought as she woke up to see flat land through the glass pane. The bus had stopped. People filed out for tea. Although she wanted it as well, she did not dare move until Sudeep did. Her first long journey in the bus had gradually begun to frighten her. The sunlight falling on Sudeep's face woke him up too.

'We should have some tea,' Sudeep said. 'Do you want anything else?'

'Nothing but tea till we reach your home,' Renu replied. 'I'd like to wash my face as well.' Renu went first to the tap in front of the shop. Sudeep sat at one of the tables inside. When Renu reached him, she found tea as well as semolina pudding in front of her. She looked puzzled.

'Eat,' Sudeep almost ordered. 'You have a long day ahead of you. On a journey you should eat when you get the chance.'

Renu did not object.

'Perhaps three hours to the Nepal border, then we cross over to India,' Sudeep said, 'then five more hours to Darjeeling.'

Renu ate in anticipation, and imagined what the city she had always wanted to visit looked like.

Sudeep dozed on and off. Renu glued her eyes to the window, and watched miles and miles of flat ground rush past her. She saw the hills far away to the north. Beautiful to look at but hard to live in, she thought as she gazed at them. After an hour or so she realised that flat land had its own problems. Many houses stood on wooden stilts. She guessed the lower areas flooded in the monsoon. In the end she decided she would prefer to live in the hills, and felt confident that Darjeeling would not disappoint her. Sudeep had pointed out where the city lay, far away among the green mountains.

A few rows in front, two men chatted in an animated way.

In fact they had kept up their conversation from the moment they entered the bus the previous evening. Renu saw that one had a newspaper in his hand. He was saying something about Kakervitta, the destination Renu would soon reach. The mention of it woke up Sudeep. He rubbed his eyes, yawned, and listened.

'A lot of people are taking girls over to India and selling them,' one said, 'even through Kakervitta.'

'How do you know?'

'Just read here.' A short pause followed.

'Hmm! That happened just a few days ago.'

'Yes, the police suspected the man. He looked too old to pose as the girl's husband. He could have said he was her father. They caught both of them. They sent the man to prison.'

'What did they do with the girl?'

'I don't know.'

Renu saw Sudeep turn pale. He coughed a bit, and pretended not to care.

'Nowadays, police suspect any couple without children,' continued one.

'Hard luck for you. I have three, you have none,' joked the other.

'So far I haven't had to cross over to India with my wife!'

'You may need to soon, get a child quickly!'

Sudeep squirmed in his seat, and shut his eyes. Renu wished the men would stop talking.

Kakervitta! As soon as the bus halted, the coolies swarmed around it like bees. Sudeep went out, and beckoned to one lad in tattered clothes to get his suitcase out. The youth climbed up to the roof and lowered it to Sudeep. Sudeep dusted the cover, and turned to Renu. 'Let's go, they'll check our baggage there.' Sudeep pointed to the check post. The youth who had lowered his suitcase followed Sudeep. He gave the boy two rupees.

'Too little,' complained the youth. 'Everyone gives five!'

'But you agreed for two!'

'I didn't.'

'You did.'

'Oh, I'll give him three rupees more,' Renu said. 'I can't stand the argument.'

Sudeep took out one rupee, and threw it to the youth. The

135

lad went away. Renu did not like her first experience of Kakervitta either.

Renu stood in line after Sudeep. The customs officer went through each bag or suitcase, and put a chalk mark on the outside when he had finished. The process irritated Sudeep. He opened his suitcase even before the officer came to him. The officer just looked, scribbled on the cover, and told him to go through. Sudeep promptly packed up and left. Renu put her bag in front of the officer.

'Open it, open it,' he said. 'Have you never travelled before?' Renu fumbled at the zipper.

'A new bag, what's in it?'

'Nothing,' replied Renu.

'Perhaps something, we have to look!' Renu struggled to keep her temper. Out came her modest clothes, the old shoulder bag, the New Testament, and her purse. The officer looked into her purse, and gave it back to her.

'All right, you can go.' The officer put a chalk mark on her new bag. Renu resented it.

She went through the 'U' shaped metal gate that allowed only one person at a time, and looked for Sudeep. Sudeep had disappeared!

He must have gone looking for a taxi, thought Renu.

She waited for a few confused minutes. A lot of old vehicles and auto-rickshaws stood to the south-east of the barrier she had just crossed. She did not see Sudeep there either. She looked back again towards the customs officer and the barrier.

Suddenly, she heard an auto-rickshaw start. Putt, putt, putt! The auto-rickshaw turned around, and swerved past her. She recognised the brown suitcase, the trousers, and the shoes. The face was hidden by the low roof of the vehicle.

'Sudeep,' she cried, 'Sudeep!' The auto-rickshaw sped away. 'Stop him!' she screamed and burst into tears.

The customs officer approached her, then a policeman.

'What's the matter?' one of them asked.

'He's run away, he's left me and run away!' Renu wept.

'Come with us to the office,' the policeman told her. 'We'll have to investigate this.'

'I thought she behaved strangely,' she heard the customs officer say.

Renu looked once more at the green hills where her anticipated future home lay. Then she turned around to go with the
policeman. She could still smell the pungent smoke the
speeding auto-rickshaw left behind.

CHAPTER
TEN

BACK HOME

Mother was crying. This time Renu knew her arrival home half an hour ago had caused it. Renu too cried sitting beside her mother next to the fire-place, but for a different reason altogether. That Friday evening had all the portents of turning nasty. Sanumaya did not beat Renu. She did not even pull Renu's hair. Drying her tears with the back of her hand, she blew her nose and wept quietly.

'Don't ever do this again,' Sanumaya, peering through watery eyes, scolded Renu. 'How could you go to Kathmandu when the police still had your father locked up?'

'I had to. I'd never visited the capital of our country,' Renu replied. 'Besides I've never had that much money before.' Renu felt into her new handbag, took out the purse; and, not bothering with the change, handed a hundred-rupee note to her mother.

'Only one hundred rupees?' Sanumaya asked.

'Yes, Mother, living in a lodge for three nights costs a lot in Kathmandu. Besides, I bought the black bag you see me carrying.'

'At least you've returned,' Sanumaya consoled herself. 'Quite a few from the village have gone and never come back.' Sanumaya stopped sobbing.

To cover up one lie, tell a hundred others! Renu remembered the popular proverb. Recovering from her tears, she started placing wood on the fire to help mother cook the evening meal. She had to know what had happened since she left. 'Were you very worried about me?'

'Worried? I've hardly slept the past three nights. Each time the dogs in the village barked, I thought you'd got back. Just to satisfy myself I'd peep out of the window.'

'Did you go anywhere to ask?' Renu inquired rather stealthily.

'On Wednesday morning, I went to the pastor's wife. She thought you must have gone to your relatives in Dhading. She told me to keep quiet about it for some days. I did. When someone asked me, I said you were in Dhading.'

'Well, Mother,' Renu lied again. 'I've spent three days in Kathmandu. Now I don't have to go there ever again! I saw the king's palace, the clock tower, and everything else.'

Content that her departure had hardly stirred up a rumour in the village, Renu worked at the fire-place more cheerfully. She put the kettle on the flames. Sanumaya wanted to rest. Renu saw her climb up the ladder. As darkness fell, Renu lit the kerosine lamp.

Curse the policemen and their investigation, Renu thought. I would've arrived yesterday if they hadn't detained me! She determined she would continue life as if nothing had happened. Villagers would see her take the cattle out the next day. She would deliberately take a meandering route to the pasture so that everyone could see her, and then all further suspicion would stop. She felt grateful to Esther for advising her mother to remain quiet. In a week Sanumaya would forget all about it, and so would the villagers, if some had noticed her absence.

Renu thought she heard someone walk on the courtyard outside.

'*Nani*, Sanumaya *nani*,' she heard a voice call. Renu left the fire-place and ran out.

'Oh, my wife said you had gone to Dhading,' Patrus said as he looked at Renu. 'When did you get back?'

'I did for a few days,' Renu repeated the lie. 'I returned yesterday.'

'You must've enjoyed the trip,' Patrus said. 'Things are too depressing in the village. I sent Sudeep to Darjeeling too, for a change.' Renu said nothing.

'Has your mother gone out?' Patrus asked.

'No, I'll call her.' Renu found her mother half-way down the ladder. Patrus entered the house. Renu unrolled the straw mat for him. Sanumaya sat next to Renu at the fire-place.

'I've come to talk to you both privately,' Patrus said. 'We should keep some things quiet, just praying to our Lord *Yesu* about them.'

'You must have brought good news,' Sanumaya said.

'Good news and bad,' Patrus replied. 'I'm sorry that Esther and I didn't tell you what went on in court on Wednesday. We thought Mahila would bring home the good news himself, but that didn't happen. We arrived back home about nine o'clock the night before last. I couldn't come then. Yesterday, I was so tired from the three-hour uphill climb of the previous evening and the ten-day police custody that I could hardly get out of bed. Forgive me for coming so late today . . . The court accepted bail money for Gangaram and myself, but not for Mahila.'

Three nights just to give the news! Renu thought. Now that he's free, he couldn't care less for Father. Why should he have bothered to come to us earlier?

'When Mahila beat me up some months ago, some Christians very foolishly reported the incident to the police. They'll probably question him about it, and release him. After all, I'll have to appear when they try that case. I can simply say Mahila has put things right with me.' Patrus explained. A stunned silence followed. 'Jogbir had gone with the money to bail Mahila out. He had to bring it back home unused,' Patrus continued.

'I don't understand,' Sanumaya finally spoke. 'Why do they release some people and not others? Are the two new people from Kathmandu still with Renu's father?'

'Those two and Gangaram spent Wednesday night in Trisuli and should've arrived home in Kathmandu yesterday,' Patrus said. 'Without even demanding bail from them, the court just released them. After all, they merely came as visitors.'

'What can we do now?' Sanumaya asked.

'We'll just have to wait and see. I'll send Jogbir with some money for Mahila tomorrow,' Patrus said. 'As soon as the police take Mahila to the court again, we can bail him out.' At this point Sanumaya slowly got up, and climbed the ladder. Renu had not spoken much so far. Patrus directed the conversation at her.

'We have to watch and pray, Renu, as the Bible says. Until we die and go to *Yesu* or *Yesu* comes to collect us on earth, our Christian life goes on as warfare.'

'When will Sudeep return?' Renu asked. 'You said he'd gone to Darjeeling.'

'Perhaps after a month or so. The Sunday school will miss him a lot,' Patrus replied. Just then, the ladder creaked. Sanumaya walked wearily towards Patrus.

'Please let Jogbir take this tomorrow when he visits my husband,' Sanumaya requested. 'We don't know how well they feed him. He may need it.'

'I'll give it to Jogbir for Mahila,' said Patrus examining the green hundred-rupee note. He arose, with eyes full of pity looked at Renu and Sanumaya, and walked out. Sanumaya politely went up to the door. Renu heard Patrus' *namasthe*, then the pastor's footsteps growing fainter and fainter.

I can't believe it, I can't, Renu thought to herself as she meditated on what Patrus has just said. She felt bitter that Patrus had not given the news to Mother the night he had come home free. Patrus' excuses did not satisfy her one bit, but in the light of her recent absence from the village she decided to keep those thoughts to herself.

Watching her mother's feeble form return to the low wooden stool by the fire, Renu was overcome by a strange emotion. All of a sudden, she rested her face on her knees and sobbed.

'Do not cry *nani*, Father will soon return,' Sanumaya consoled her daughter. Renu sobbed on for a while, wiped her tears and nose with the tip of her *fariah*, and finally controlled herself.

'I wasn't crying because they've kept Father. He can take care of himself.'

'Why were you crying then?' Sanumaya asked. Renu felt her eyes well up again.

'I felt so sorry you could send only one hundred rupees and not two for Father.'

'Come on,' said Mother. 'I value you more than the hundred rupees. I really do.'

***

Renu had just finished watering the cattle when she recognised Jogbir from afar. By then, she had learnt to fear every man who approached her. Of course, women hardly came to her home after her father had declared himself a Christian. She wondered what news Jogbir had this time.

He must have given the money to Father, Renu thought, the pastor promised to send it with him yesterday.

She ran excitedly to Sanumaya who lay on her bed for her afternoon nap. Sanumaya woke up, smoothed her hair a bit, and appeared at the door as Jogbir arrived. He was totally out of breath. Sanumaya and Renu greeted him. As Jogbir stood in the courtyard Renu saw his face was paler than ever before. He refused to sit on the straw mat on the verandah.

'I bring some terrible news,' he announced. 'Curse me for having to tell it.'

'He isn't dead, is he?' asked Sanumaya, and started sobbing.

'Not that bad,' Jogbir said. 'I went to meet Mahila this morning. The pastor had given me some money for him. At first, the police wouldn't allow me to see him at all. I pleaded and pleaded. Finally, a sergeant came. He said Mahila had fallen sick and that I could visit him only if I'd promise to bring people to carry him away, at the latest, tomorrow. I promised, and was given two minutes to see Mahila. Mahila couldn't move from where he lay. In a voice scarcely audible, he said they had tortured him the very night our pastor came home a free man.'

Renu began sobbing when her mother, no doubt relieved by the news that Mahila was still alive, stopped. Jogbir put his hand into his pocket, and stretched over towards Sanumaya. Sanumaya stared at the green notes.

'But I gave only one hundred; you've given me two,' Sanumaya protested.

'Oh, keep it. The other is from us. We don't know how much medication Mahila may need.'

'Shouldn't we take him to hospital?' Sanumaya suggested.

'I'll borrow the pastor's canvas camp bed, and go with four or five other men to carry Mahila out of that wretched room in the police barracks. Then we'll do as he says. We'll take him to hospital if he wants us to. If not, we'll bring him home.'

'We depend on you,' Sanumaya said. For some reason, Renu continued sobbing.

'Pray to *Yesu*. Only He can help; I'll have to go . . . Oh, I

143

nearly forgot it again,' said Jogbir, reaching to his chest under his shirt. 'Mahila whispered to me that he had guarded this with his life and wanted you to have it at all costs.' Renu took the folded copy-book, still wet with Jogbir's sweat.

'Father didn't even mention he was writing this when we met him at the police barracks,' she muttered to Mother after Jogbir had left.

***

Friday
My dear Renu:
After I left you yesterday, your lovely face appeared in front of my eyes every few minutes. That made me feel even more guilty for my past bouts of drunkenness and their consequences. I take this opportunity to apologise for the way I've treated you. I needn't repeat why I began to drink. *Yesu* has taught me to put behind all those evil memories, and ask your forgiveness, also your mother's. She can't understand me now, but explain this to her when she can.

I must admit that my attitude to the police has changed even more since yesterday. The officers here are swindlers. There's not a trace of human- ity left in them. It's a different story with the ordinary policemen. Yesterday morning when we were coming to Dhanee Gaon, the five constables who trudged with their rifles at their arms com- plained bitterly about the sub-inspector.

'That bastard and the sergeant left on horses long ago.'

'He expects the villagers to feed us. He gave us only half our daily allowance.'

'I asked him if we could just bring our batons only. We have to climb for two hours with these heavy rifles!'

Slowly I pieced together a character portrait of the sub-inspector. 'Doesn't the inspector take an interest in the case?' I asked. 'I haven't seen him at all '

'The day after they arrested you, he went on leave. If he'd stayed, he'd have sent you all home by now.'

I didn't expect any generosity from the inspector, but I realised that his assistant, in his enthusiasm for cruelty, had transgressed all normal boundaries.

Their complaints along the way revealed that those ordinary policemen too could be counted among the oppressed. After their sub-inspector and the sergeant galloped ahead of us on their horses, they poured out their hearts to us. I had not realised how much tyranny and dissatisfaction lay hidden behind their crude jokes and laughter.

The sun had set when we returned to the barracks after our visit to Dhanee Gaon. It was an exhausting anticlimax. The caricature of justice we'd witnessed had wearied us out more than the six-hour trek. The banyan tree caught my attention first. I almost felt jealous that I should find someone else taking the seat I normally occupied under its shade. I turned to Gangaram just behind me.

'I see some people under the tree.'

'I do too,' Gangaram replied, 'perhaps some other victims the police have found!' The pastors and I strained our eyes to get a glimpse of the visitors. The newcomers were staring at us too. All of a sudden, one stood up and approached us.

'*Namasthe*, pastor *dai!*'

'Oh, now I know who it is!' exclaimed Gangaram. 'Sam and Bharat! What brings you here?'

'What brings us here? The sad news of your arrest of course!' We folded our hands to each other in greetings.

'When we arrived, we wanted to talk to the inspector. They said he had gone away on leave. The sub-inspector had left for Dhanee Gaon with all of you. One policeman advised us to meet the *CDO*.'

'Did you?'

'Yes indeed. Like a bulldog, the *CDO* barked at us. He asked us why we had come. To meet our friends, we said. He asked if we also worshipped *Yesu*. We said we did. Then the *CDO* ordered his bodyguard to arrest us!'

'What?' Gangaram shrieked. 'Oh, Nepal, Nepal!'

'Yes, we also share your fate now,' replied Sam. 'We remained a long while in the room. Then the sentry allowed us to sit under the tree. We've waited for you.'

'Oh brothers,' sighed Gangaram. 'What a visit!'

Wednesday

Yesterday the police took Sam and Bharat to Dhanee Gaon for the villagers to testify against them. You must have watched everything in amazement because our village hadn't even seen the two men before. They had come to Trisuli district for the first time. However, that procedure completed all that the police needed to hand us five over to the court. Sergeant Lal appeared as we sipped our morning tea. 'Your happy day has arrived,' Lal said. 'Some of you may eat dinner at home tonight.'

'And probably travel to and from the court for years after that,' Gangaram replied. 'You policemen surely know how to make our lives miserable.'

'Just become Hindus again and there'll be no more trouble,' Lal remarked.

'Or allow us to choose our own religion as most civilised nations in the world do and no more extra work for you,' Gangaram retorted.

'Yes, this case has embarrassed us,' Sergeant Lal admitted. 'Most people ask why we've arrested religious people. All because of the pig-headed sub-inspector!' This outburst came more from frustration than from the character of the officer accused. I feel certain both the sergeant and the sub-inspector had plotted together.

'Before you go to court, you still have to sign some papers,' the sergeant changed the subject. 'These testify that we've given you food during your stay with us.'

'But mightn't we be back here tonight? We can sign then, can't we?' Gangaram asked doubtfully.

'Oh no, we've dealt with cases like this so often that we can always predict what will happen.' The sergeant held out the open file to Patrus first.

'We fasted one meal,' Patrus remarked, 'but you put us down as eating that one too!'

'Oh, don't bother about that,' Gangaram remarked with a twinkle. 'Don't make it complicated for their accounts!' I signed last of all. After the sergeant left, I found myself humming. Freedom so close, I thought, I'll eat at home tonight!

Esther had sent news that another man from Gangaram's church had arrived in Dhanee Gaon. He had brought enough money for bail. I imagined myself relating our ten-day experience to Sanumaya and you around the fire-place, taking out the cattle to the pastures on the Tarachuli summit, and gazing at the river flowing down the valley so peacefully. I pictured you going to school again, Sanumaya cautiously entering the church for the first time. Above all, I saw myself walk home as a free man.

Inside the court that day I noticed the captions that adorned the walls of the waiting area. Just above the entrance into the court chamber, I read aloud, 'He who gives a bribe sins even more than he who takes it.'

'At least someone had the right ideas,' Patrus pointed out the text to Gangaram.

'He certainly did,' Gangaram replied. 'I only wish they'd put it into practice.' I did not respond, but began reading the other captions.

Looking out, I saw Jogbir and another person

approach the court building. 'Do you know the other man?' I asked Patrus.

'No.'

'Why of course, it's Madan,' Gangaram replied, 'a deacon from my church. He must have brought the money.'

Sam and Bharat went out to greet the newcomer. The rest waited for them to enter the building.

'Why! I sent messages asking you not to meet us,' Gangaram warned. 'Look what happened to Bharat and Sam!'

'I expect different behaviour in a court,' Madan replied. 'I won't go to the police barracks if I sense danger.'

'Very wise of you,' Gangaram said. 'Although you see the constables sitting and chatting on the grass, they won't harm you. It's the others at the top we have to fear.' Jogbir grinned and stood on one side while the conversation continued. After a while, Gangaram took Madan out for a private briefing.

I heard Sergeant Lal mention my name in the room next to the court chamber, and wondered what was going on. The gong at the barracks had sounded twelve long ago. After the sergeant left, I saw Gangaram enter and complain at the delay.

'You've waited for the last ten days, why rush now?' the official behind the desk protested.

'We have waited only very reluctantly,' Gangaram remonstrated.

'Typical of our pastor,' Sam laughed. I smiled. The man I had seen on Buddha's birthday and the previous Wednesday appeared again. Patrus found that he worked as the court *subbha*. He, the prosecutor, the sergeant, and the sub-inspector regularly met for tea. The *subbha* entered the court chamber. Patrus went into the side-room where Gangaram was still chatting to the court official.

'Don't we have a judge in the court?' I heard

Patrus ask.

'He went for his daughter's wedding, and hasn't come back.'

'Can the *subbha* decide the case then?'

'Of course not. He's just the court administrator. He'll do the necessary for you to pay bail and go home.'

The *subbha* called for Gangaram. Through the court door I observed the same question and answer pattern I had experienced twice before. The administrator wrote down everything the pastor said, read it back to him, and asked him to sign the document. Next Patrus went in, then Sam, and finally Bharat. Each person took an hour or more. Jogbir and Madan went to the shops, and returned with a kettle of tea, glasses, and biscuits. I wondered when the *subbha* would call me.

After Bharat finished, the administrator didn't call anyone. Instead he looked at his file, read, and re-read some documents. I stood at the door in anticipation. The *subbha* noticed me. 'Who are you? Mahila?' asked the administrator. 'We won't have your hearing today. I've received notification that the police need more time with you.'

I turned around to Patrus in dismay.

'But I don't understand this, sir,' Gangaram protested. 'How can the police finish with Bharat and Sam and not with Mahila? They arrested him right at the beginning with us.'

'Let them decide that,' the administrator replied. 'The court can't deal with a case not fully prepared.'

'What will happen to him, then?'

'They'll take him back to custody tonight. They will bring him here when they feel ready. You know he beat up a man some time back. The police want to look into that too.'

'But he beat *me*,' Patrus replied, 'not anyone else. We have forgiven and forgotten. Why do you continue to dig it up?'

'Ask the police.' The administrator left for tea. He said he'd announce his decision after half an hour.

'Well, we have all the money to buy your freedom, Mahila,' said Gangaram angrily, 'but the culprits have snared you again. Only *Yesu* can help you now.'

'I know,' I replied.

'I'll get all the Christians in Kathmandu fasting and praying,' Gangaram said. 'What can I do? For the Christians, the *Rana* rule hasn't ended.'

'Oh, don't worry,' I reassured him. 'They may respect a military man.'

'An *ex-military* man,' Patrus corrected. 'Don't rely on that, Mahila. Only trust the Lord.' With dejected faces, Sam, Bharat, Madan, and Jogbir listened.

'Poor Mahila,' Patrus sighed, but his joy at being free himself came through.

The administrator returned after forty-five minutes. 'I've dealt very leniently with all of you,' he began. 'I could have locked all of you up indefinitely.'

'How?' asked Gangaram.

'I could have tried you for treason against the king of Nepal himself!'

'Why?'

'All Nepal regards the king as the incarnation of god *Bishnu*. You Christians worship neither our gods nor our king.'

'Even His Majesty wouldn't go along with such superstition,' Gangaram protested. 'This is your own fabrication!'

'Well, at least now you understand how I could try you all for treason, and then you wouldn't be let out even on bail. I'll at least accept that from you.'

'So kind of you,' replied Gangaram, 'also equally ingenious.' Patrus shoved Gangaram gently to keep him quiet.

'Well, I've decided that Gangaram*ji* and Pa-trus*ji* can pay Rs. 3780 each. You will both have to appear in the court in a month's time. Bharat and Sam needn't pay anything. They were just on the receiving end of the outburst of the *CDO* who wasn't in a very good mood that day.' Jogbir and Madan walked to the office to make the needed payment for the two pastors. The administrator disappeared through the back door.

The cobblestones through the Trisuli bazaar sounded hostile as I trod on them again. This time, only I walked between the four policemen; the two pastors and the rest were following free. I saw all eyes in the bazaar focus on me. Strangely, I was totally unmoved, and kept looking straight ahead. With my friends behind, I soon entered the room I'd hoped I'd left for ever.

The two pastors left the overcoats, which the quartermaster had lent us, lying on the stocks. Bharat and Sam, who had just come for a day visit, had nothing to pack. Gangaram folded his sleeping bag into a separate pouch. Madan took hold of the pastor's air bag.

'Patrus will forgive us for not going to Dhanee Gaon tonight. We'll stay in a lodge in Trisuli and catch the first bus tomorrow morning,' Gangaram said apologetically.

'I can understand. The three-hour walk up there would kill you!'

'It hasn't so far, Patrus. I'll visit you again in a month,' Gangaram replied. 'You still have my shaver. Meanwhile, I'll keep my beard till my wife sees it, the only souvenir I have for her this time! Now let's pray before we leave.'

One after another, all prayed for me, that *Yesu's* presence might comfort me, that I might continue to trust the Lord, that the Lord might keep me firm in faith, that He might save me from sickness and injuries . . .

'Sadly, we've to leave you now, Mahila, but we

leave our hearts behind.' Gangaram's eyes filled with tears. Patrus stared restlessly at the floor. He seemed to be in a hurry to get home.

'God will take care of me, only remember me in your prayers,' I assured them. Each embraced me.

I watched them file out of the room. They walked past the banyan tree, and turned left. Gangaram walked last in the line. As he turned the corner, he lifted up his hand. I waved back.

Frowning at me, the sentry came to lock the door he had left open till then. I quickly realised my luck had run out. Plucking up courage, I asked for a lamp. Surprisingly he brought a lighted one immediately. The gong struck six. Supper was at least three hours away. I didn't want to read. I tried to pray, but the disappointment of the day distracted me too much. My thoughts turned to you – how you would cry bitterly when you saw our pastor a free man and not me.

I made my bed more comfortable with more layers of blankets and overcoats. I wanted to lie down, rest and forget reality, but decided to attend to my diary first . . . Well, I've brought you up to date. Oh, I feel so sleepy . . .

***

The next day, with the contents of the diary still swirling in her head, Renu tidied up her home in anticipation of seeing her father back. She swept every corner of the house twice. She applied the cow dung and red clay mixture to both the floors. She put a bunch of rhododendrons into a vase she had improvised from an old ink bottle. Sanumaya had decided that she would sleep with Renu from that night. So Renu made her father's bed five times over. She just had one sheet at her disposal, but tried to cover the bed with it in the most attractive way. The quilt cover, which she had washed the day before immediately after receiving news of her father's probable home-coming, now felt crisp and dry after a day in the *Jestha* sun. The pillow she used was Father's favourite – it had a green border with a yellow moon in the middle. She folded the quilt until it looked like a gigantic sausage, and placed it to the side against the wall. She then went on to prepare the other bed for Mother and herself. She managed to make a little more room by pulling the wooden cot six inches away from the wall. She extended the cotton mattress into the gap, and congratulated herself on the slightly larger bed she had produced. She also toyed with the idea that Mother and she would serve as Father's bodyguards, ready to run on errands whenever he wanted them to do something.

Father, back home! thought Renu. Soon, she started humming a tune.

Father did not arrive by noon or sunset. Sanumaya and Renu wondered what could have gone wrong. They lit the small kerosine lamp. Sanumaya had decided to cook for three. She busied herself at the fire-place while Renu went in and out of the house to the cattle shed in the hope of getting a glimpse of four or five men carrying her father.

Get a glimpse, she did, finally, in the hazy dusk. Jogbir led the way. His right hand steadied the frame of the camp bed. Two men carried it on on each side, level with their waists. Another clutched the frame at the end opposite to Jogbir. Renu shouted the news to her mother. Sanumaya came out to the courtyard, covered her head with the tip of her *fariah*, and watched quietly as the canvas bed the men carried drew near. In a few minutes, Mahila, her husband, lay moaning and groaning in front of her. Renu could scarcely recognise her father. He had dwindled to one half of himself. However, his hands and feet appeared double the normal size. She noticed clotted blood on some of the finger tips. She had longed to see her father, but not in this state!

'What have they done to you? Oh, what have they done?' Sanumaya stroked her husband's hair and started weeping. Renu tried to comfort Mother by placing her hand on her shoulder, but broke down too. Jogbir and the men who had carried Mahila stood silent and dazed.

'We just couldn't come earlier,' Jogbir explained after a while. 'The sun was shining too brightly for the upward climb. We rested at the tea shop down below.'

'Didn't you take him to hospital?' In a broken voice, Sanumaya reminded Jogbir of her suggestion the day before.

'We wanted to,' Jogbir replied, 'but couldn't persuade Mahila to agree. He said the police had beaten him up very badly. In a few days he'd recover, he assured us. He just longed to come back home.'

'We've made a bed for him upstairs,' Renu said, controlling herself. 'Can you please carry him there?'

'We can, but will Mahila agree?' Jogbir asked. 'Even a small jolt must cause him terrible pain.' Jogbir went to Mahila, and in an unusually loud voice, asked if he would sleep upstairs. Drying her eyes, Renu watched her father. For some time, he did not respond. Then feebly he nodded his head backward and forward, a 'yes' for sure. Renu smiled faintly, happy that her preparations from the morning would not be wasted. Her father had arrived at last.

Jogbir decided that the best way to take Mahila up would be to carry the camp bed he lay on up the ladder. Little did he realise that this would prove the steepest hill for the group that had faithfully carried Mahila so far. Renu stood on the top floor with the kerosine lamp flickering in her left hand. She kept her right hand free in case they required her to lift a bit too. Two men squatted on the top rung, two lifted the middle of the bed from below, two helped at Mahila's feet. Renu shut her eyes as she heard her father moan in agony. Sanumaya sobbed. Finally, the men managed to slip the camp cot through the opening for the ladder on the top floor. Renu sighed in relief. Transferring Mahila from the camp cot to the bed proved easier. Jogbir directed the men to lift the cot to the level of the bed. Then they gently rolled Mahila on to the sheet Renu had arranged so carefully. Jogbir covered Mahila up to his chin with the quilt.

'Let him sleep,' Jogbir advised Sanumaya and Renu. 'When he wakes up, give him a paste of *dahl* and rice. He'll recover fast here. This room isn't so smoky as the one below.'

One by one the men went down the creaking ladder, out to the courtyard.

'We have to go home, now,' Jogbir said to Sanumaya and Renu. 'At least Mahila has freed himself from the clutches of the police. All of us will have to nurse him back to health.' The women kept silent, but gratefully folded their hands in *namasthe*. The courtyard, noisy till a few minutes ago, was soon empty apart from Renu and Sanumaya. Both expressed surprise that neither Patrus nor Esther were present to welcome Mahila.

'At least Sushila should have come,' said Renu, 'but would she know better than her parents?'

'Oh, don't worry,' comforted Sanumaya. 'This is life. They say, "Tell your joys to all, but keep the sorrows to yourself".'

Going up, Renu pulled at the wick of the kerosine lamp, and made its flame even smaller. She placed it on the window sill below her father's bed. During the course of cooking dinner, she climbed up several times. Her father lay sound asleep. Sanumaya and Renu decided to have their meal first. They finished washing up around ten o'clock. When Renu and Sanumaya climbed up to sleep, Mahila stirred a bit.

'Father do you want to eat anything?' Renu almost shouted. Mahila opened his eyes for a while, looked at Renu but could not focus his eyes on her.

'Back home!' He whispered. In the seconds that followed, her father fell asleep again. The kerosine lamp, which had flickered for a while for lack of oil, went out completely.

CHAPTER
ELEVEN

DOWNHILL

Four weary weeks had passed since they had carried Renu's father home. Both Sanumaya and Renu realised his health was going steadily downhill. Mahila had shown signs of improvement the first week. The swelling in the hands and the legs had subsided. Renu, silently shedding tears, washed away the clotted blood on the fingers and toes with a handkerchief soaked in warm water. Sanumaya just did not have the courage to look at those wounds and the bruises on his back. For some days she wept and cursed both *Ram* and *Yesu* for allowing her husband the ordeal. Both the gods were impotent as far as she was concerned, and she chided Renu for worshipping the latter. Renu did not know how to answer her mother. Instead, she evaded her questions by busying herself in nursing Father.

Why did you allow it, *Yesu*, why? She must have asked in her mind a million times.

For a few days, Renu noticed blood in his urine. With her mother, she sighed in relief when the blood disappeared. Faintly but coherently, Mahila talked.

'I remember the night they tortured me only too well,' he began. 'When my friends went out free, I wrote for a while; but I was too disappointed to do anything else. I lay down to rest and relied on the sentry to wake me up at meal time. Since I felt thoroughly exhausted, sleep came quite easily. When I awoke, I thought I heard not one but two sentries.

"Get up, you, husband of a cow!" ordered one.

"Come on, don't delay!" thundered the other.

"Meal time already?" I asked.

"Meal for you, husband of a cow, we have a meal for you!" a voice replied. Then a torch light shone into my eyes for a few seconds. It took me a while to focus my eyes in the dark. Both the sergeant and the sub-inspector have come, I thought, they could just as well have sent constables for me. Still not knowing why they'd come, I stood up. Perhaps I'd overslept and annoyed the cook in the kitchen. I fumbled in the dark for my shoes.

"You don't need shoes, you bastard, come on!" I felt the men grab both my arms and open the door. Outside, stood other constables and policemen.

As the men marched me out, my feet automatically headed for the kitchen.

"This way," shouted one, grabbing my arm tighter.

It took me a few seconds to realise the destiny that awaited me. I must have wailed like a jackal when I realised they were taking me to the torture chamber.'

Without emotion, he described the agonies he had experienced: pins thrust into his fingers and toes, chilli powder on his private parts, scourging with nettles, cigarette burns, hanging upside down and naked from the ceiling, and further beatings.

'I don't remember how long I hung,' Mahila had said feebly. 'My head started to ache terribly after some time. Then I must have fainted. Next, I woke up in the room where they'd thrown me.'

'Tell no more, Father, tell no more,' Renu had begged, but Mahila did not have anything else to talk about. She was a bit weary hearing the same story over and over again. Mother and she shuddered when Mahila screamed as nightmares shattered his sleep. He scarcely swallowed a spoonful of rice and *dahl*. Renu could not even force down half a spoon that morning. Mahila just vomited whatever entered his mouth. Then he complained of a severe headache and itching all over. With the help of her mother, Renu tried to force a paracetamol tablet into his mouth. Mahila vomited that too, and went to sleep. His breathing was jerky and noisy. He seemed to gasp at times. Renu burst into tears, and ran to report the deterioration to the pastor.

Patrus came to Mahila, prayed, shook his head in despair, and looked lovingly at the form he had helped baptise six weeks previously. The day after they had carried Mahila home, Patrus too had seen no need of hospital treatment. The bruises and the blue spots on his body were many, but he had confidence in the nursing Mahila received at home. He assured Sanumaya and Renu that Mahila would walk within ten days. He almost boasted of the accuracy of his prediction after the first week. Leaning on the pillow between himself and the wall, Mahila had taken a bit of food. However, Patrus found Mahila worse on his next visit. The ten days anticipated for Mahila's recovery had lengthened to twenty-nine. He had become worse.

'The greatest thing about our God,' Patrus explained to Renu, 'is that we can't dictate to Him. We can pray for healing, but He may heal or not heal. He does as He pleases.'

That does not help us now, does it? Renu thought to herself.

That noon Patrus felt strongly that they should take Mahila to the hospital.

'He looks too weak for three or four hours on the shoulders of men,' Sanumaya broke in softly. 'Perhaps we could call a doctor here.'

'Tomorrow, I'll have to appear in the court at Trisuli. Pastor Gangaram too will come from Kathmandu. After the business in the court, we'll try to get a doctor to come here with us.' Patrus tried to give all the hope he could. Renu felt a bit better. She regretted having to call the pastor each time before he would come. Esther had not turned up more than once after Mahila's home-coming.

'Mahila's stopped eating. He gasps for breath. His symptoms frighten me,' Patrus concluded standing up from Renu's bed. 'We should have a time of fasting and prayer the whole of this Saturday. Anyway, we'll get the doctor tomorrow.' As Patrus left, Renu felt totally alone.

Renu had plenty of time to meditate on the past month. Her father's present state had brought some compensations as well. Gradually, the villagers heard why Mahila lay sick in bed. The more vitriolic ones cursed the police.

'It's none of their business whether Mahila turns a Christian or a Muslim,' said one. 'They could have handed him over to the court. What did the bastards want to prove?'

'Such atrocities didn't happen even during the *Rana* rule,' complained a more enlightened villager. 'Now supposedly we

159

enjoy this farce of a democracy.'

'If Mahila had offered even more money, he wouldn't have suffered!'

'Mahila has no grudge against his persecutors, I can't understand it!'

'Christians run schools in Kathmandu. The highest officials break their necks to get their children into them. Why beat up Christians here?'

'They'd have drunk and gambled with Mahila. He changed for the better. That made them furious . . .'

How the tide has turned, thought Renu, five weeks ago these same people were testifying against my father!

The visit of the *Pradhan Panch* had surprised Renu the most. He wanted to ask Mahila's forgiveness. When he found Mahila could not respond, he wept in front of Sanumaya. He asked her to use for Mahila's medication the three hundred rupees she had borrowed from his wife. The women folk begged Sanumaya and Renu to use the village tap again. When Mahila failed to improve, the visits of the villagers dwindled too; but Renu could not count a single household that had not sent someone to express sympathy. Never before had the non-Christians so united with the Christians.

The next morning, Renu was alarmed to find she felt extremely drowsy. Although she had already urinated twice in the early hours of the morning, she went down the ladder to the back of the house again. There she vomited a watery, sour fluid. Her head ached. Dawn was already breaking, but she went back to bed. Nursing her father gave her and her mother the excuse to get up late. For days Renu had not taken the cattle out to pasture. The buffalo and the cow, as if realising what was going on, were content with straw and water. The cow still gave a trickle of milk. The women tried in vain to force it on Mahila. Renu's troubled mind began to worry about her own health as well as her father's deterioration.

When Renu finally forced herself to get up, she found that there was no urgency; she could have slept longer if she had wished. Mahila lay asleep, gasping and noisy. She milked the cow, and after setting aside some milk for Father, made tea for Mother and herself. He had not eaten anything the day before. When he woke up, he did not want to eat any that day either.

All this looked ominous. Renu wished her father would pester her, ask her to make delicacies of all kinds, make her read from the New Testament. Mahila did none of these. Instead, his eyes remained closed for most of the time. When they opened, he just blinked for a few seconds, and fell asleep again. His wounds had now healed. There was nothing serious to see. Sanumaya and Renu wondered just what had gone wrong.

However, that day offered some hope. They remembered the promise Patrus had made the day before. They counted the hours for the doctor and the two pastors to arrive. Although Renu had not eaten much, she had got over the strange symptoms of the morning. She imagined herself busy serving the guests tea, and visualised the doctor feeling her father's pulse. She volunteered to take the cattle out that noon. Somehow, the day looked much brighter.

The cattle went to exactly the same spot where she had quarrelled with Father for calling her mother a 'child eater'. She regretted the harsh language she had used. She was afraid that Father would never again sit there with her and hear softer words. Her resentment at having to drop out of school disappeared.

I will fulfil my ambition, she vowed, I will become a nurse!

She tried to forget her ill-fated elopement with Sudeep. After all, everyone makes some mistakes in life; and he had proved a scoundrel quite early! She had been spared the agony of spending her life with a man who did not really love her. But ... She felt herself choke. She relived that dreadful event at the Indian border. She would never be the same again. Darjeeling? Sudeep? Forget them – life must go on! The rigours of Dhanee Gaon had trained her to bounce back and get on. The subsistence farming, the failed monsoon rains, the sun parching the sown seeds, the former drunken life of her father, the tears of her mother had given her a resolute will. But ...

The Trisuli river flowing without a care gave her hope. It had done so for centuries! It had cut through countless valleys, swept away innumerable boulders, irrigated millions of paddy fields, illumined thousands of homes – though mostly in Kathmandu! The river looked the prettiest in adversity. May I succeed in the midst of these very adversities! wished Renu. She looked up at the blue sky overhead, down again at the blue waters of the river. Suddenly, she found herself humming a tune.

When Renu arrived home with the cattle, she realised she had stayed longer at the pasture than she wished. She needed a watch! She determined the first salary she earned as a nurse would go towards purchasing one. She blamed herself for the daydreaming, but Father had not demanded much attention anyway. Sanumaya said that he had awakened once or twice, but fallen asleep again. Renu quickly climbed up the ladder, and verified what Mother had said. She did not feel guilty any more.

After the sun set, Renu lit the small kerosine lamp, and put it below her father's bed on the window sill. She had done so every night, and knew just how low a wick conserved kerosine. Mahila opened his eyes once when the pale yellow light approached him.

'Won't you eat anything, Father?' Renu asked softly. Mahila shut his eyes in response, and kept them shut. Lovingly, Renu arranged the quilt that covered him. Not having any spares, Renu could not wash the pillow case and the quilt cover. Father had not recovered as she expected. They looked a dirty yellow.

Any time now the doctor should arrive, thought Renu. She made sure any draught through the joints in the wooden window panes did not blow the lamp out, and went down to help Mother in the kitchen.

Renu and Sanumaya were eating when they heard a noise outside.

'Renu,' a voice called. At least Patrus had arrived. Quickly washing her right hand on the ashes of the fire-place, she rushed to open the door. Sanumaya did the same, and hid the dishes and the utensils they had just used.

'No doctor would climb the hill, Renu,' Patrus replied rather sheepishly as soon as the door opened, 'but our health assistant sahib has kindly come, also Pastor Gangaram.' Renu did a grateful *namasthe* to the three men at the door, and asked them in. By now, Sanumaya had come with the lamp.

'Upstairs,' she said feebly.

'How is he today?' asked Patrus.

'He hasn't eaten anything. Although his breathing was

162

heavy and jerky, he's slept the whole day. Once or twice he blinked,' Renu answered. Renu had seen Pastor Gangaram only once before her visit to her father in police custody. He remained unusually quiet that night, and followed the health assistant up the ladder. Supplementing the light of the lamp with hers, Sanumaya stood close to Mahila's leg. Gangaram kept his torch light ready. Thank God, Renu said to herself. The 'doctor' has arrived.

The health assistant opened the buttons on Mahila's chest, and put his stethoscope on it. Gangaram shone the torch light. Mahila did not stir as the cold instrument touched his skin. The health assistant listened. He shook his head. He took Mahila's wrist, felt the pulse, and looked at his watch. He shook his head again. He looked at Mahila's eyes. He shook his head yet once more, and turned to Patrus.

'The pupils are wide and fixed! I fear your effort to get me here was too late,' the health assistant said looking sternly at Mahila. 'The patient is already dead!'

A thud! Sanumaya had collapsed on the floor. Renu ran to her mother's side, and picked the lamp up from the floor. She put her hand under Mother's neck, and tried to lift her head up. Then she broke down sobbing, and was forced to lower her mother's head to the floor.

'Why has all this to happened to me? Why?' she cried, covering both her eyes.

'Let's get the mother to this bed,' the health assistant suggested. He, Patrus, and Gangaram took over. After they had lain Sanumaya on the bed, the health assistant took the pillow away from her head, and put it under her legs instead.

'We have to open the window a bit,' said the health assistant. Sitting on the bed at her father's feet, Renu continued weeping, almost in a howl. Patrus pushed the lamp at the window sill closer to the wall, and opened the left wooden pane slightly.

'What is there to say?' the health assistant continued. 'The government has built a hospital just three hours away. People wait till the last moment.'

'In this case,' replied Patrus, 'we didn't suspect anything serious. The police beat and tortured him. He seemed better at the end of the first week. He stopped passing blood in his urine, and we all thought he'd recover.'

'If the police beat him hanging him upside down for over an hour, probably two things could've happened – either brain or kidney haemorrhage. But I'm not sure. I'm not sure at all ... Brain haemorrhage would've killed him quicker. Blood in the urine makes me think they must've damaged his kidneys. The patient passed blood in his urine as long as the kidney still functioned. Later he must've urinated less and less, and gradually stopped altogether as the waste inside attacked the kidneys even more – I'm not a doctor, even a doctor couldn't be sure. If what I think is correct, ceasing to pass blood in the urine was a bad sign in this case. The patient was actually getting worse. The kidneys were failing. Only very special treatment in time could've saved his kidneys and his life.'

'So much for the entertainment the police get out of torture!' said Gangaram, who had remained quiet so far.

'I cannot believe it,' the health assistant shook his head. 'The hospital I work in lies so close to the police barracks. So far no one has even told me of the tortures that go on there.'

'We can testify to them,' said Gangaram. 'Did I tell you what they did to the woman fit to be their grandmother?'

'You did . . . sorry,' the health assistant apologised, 'I arrived too late to do anything!' By now Renu had knelt on the floor beside her father's bed, and, whining and sobbing alternately, begun to caress his feet beneath the quilt.

The health assistant turned his attention on Sanumaya. 'She'll recover, she's just had a terrible shock.'

'I'll stay here with her and Renu. Patrus*ji* will take you to his home,' Gangaram announced, looking at them both. 'We can't leave Renu alone like this.'

'After the health assistant sahib has eaten something, I'll send Esther and Sushila here,' Patrus replied. 'You have your sleeping bag, don't you?'

'I have,' said Gangaram, ' but I don't think I'll get much sleep tonight. Ask Esther to bring some snacks and tea.'

'I shall,' replied Patrus. 'My head aches if I don't sleep, and we have the funeral tomorrow.'

'We'll go down to the fire-place soon after Renu's mother wakes up,' Gangaram replied.

'She may not wake up till quite late,' the health assistant

replied. 'She fainted just at her bed time.'

'No matter,' said Gangaram, 'we'll survive the night some-how.'

By the time Renu lifted her head and wiped away her tears, the 'doctor' she relied on had disappeared with Patrus.

***

Ever since she understood the meaning of death, Renu had feared funerals. She could not pinpoint exactly what scared her; but every time she saw mourners processing to the cremation site on top of Tarachuli it depressed her. Perhaps it was because she had witnessed her uncle's funeral when she was barely nine years old.

How clearly she remembered it! Father had woken up early that morning and gone to cut firewood in the jungle. She herself lay huddled in the quilt of her bed while Mother, ready to start her day's work, was sipping tea on the verandah. Just then news of her uncle's sudden death had arrived. Her mother dropped her glass of tea. At that sound Renu, half naked, ran down the ladder and outside. Mother appeared depressed but was not weeping. Uncle's home was in the next village. Renu had hardly ever seen him. Mother explained that they would now have to stop eating food with salt, and manage with only one meal each evening until the funeral was over. That afternoon Renu had followed Mother to the home of her widowed aunt and watched everything with childish curiosity.

She noted each ritual of the funeral. The deceased was left on his bed for three days until all the relatives gathered. They arrived in all shapes and sizes, from far and near. Faces never seen before were introduced as cousins, aunts, and maternal uncles. Some wept, others did not; but all ended up talking stoically of the realities of life and praising the virtues of the deceased. The more Renu listened the more her dead uncle seemed to have been a saint who distributed sweets to children like her. If only she had visited Uncle's home more often while he lived! However, by the third day, Renu was tired of all the talking, and even more of taking food without salt. She wished the funeral was over.

On the actual day of the funeral, *lamas* came to perform the necessary ceremonies. Renu observed three attend to her uncle. The main *lama* sat at her uncle's head, and recited things she did not understand. Then taking a brass implement similar to miniature dumb-bells, he wound uncle's long pig-tail on it. Then, to Renu's horror, he slowly pulled out the tuft of hair. She learned later that by doing this the *lama* had saved her uncle from going to hell.

Then followed the beautifying of the deceased. Fascinated, Renu watched the sons-in-law applying make-up on her uncle for his last journey up the hill. They undressed him and then wrapped his body in a long saffron cloth. They forced the body into a squatting position, tied his hands and feet, and applied a variety of creams. They oiled and combed his hair, painted his eye-lashes, powdered his face, and garlanded his neck. In the end Uncle looked startlingly handsome yet frightful, as if ready to get up and dance, as masked men did during festivals.

Next, the body was placed in a gigantic copper pot, and carried on the shoulders of four men by means of poles that went through the rings on the side of the vessel. A large portrait of Buddha on decorated cloth led the procession. The head *lama* followed. In his hand he held the brass implement that pulled out the pig-tail. It had been tied to the body with strips of clothing. The mourning relatives, men and women, followed. Renu held firmly onto the hand of a maternal uncle she had befriended just the day before. Uncle's reputation in the village had brought in a lot of spectators who trod the winding dirt path. A cloud of dust enveloped the mourners. The crowd inched its way to an isolated spot to the left of the Tarachuli summit. The innumerable heaps of stones testified that the Tamangs had put their dead to rest here since time immemorial.

At the site, a freshly dug pit covered with a platform of firewood awaited the deceased. The *lamas* began to read from their holy books. Relatives offered money which the *lamas* had waved in front of Uncle and put into their common bag.

The cremation followed. The sons of the deceased lit the fire, and his sons-in-law helped to keep it going. Realising what was about to happen, Renu's maternal uncle had mercifully taken her for a long walk. Even so, she felt sick at the sound of the crackling fire and the stench of the burning flesh. When she got back, she saw a pile of stones as tall as herself over the pit where Uncle's ashes lay buried. She wondered how Uncle had responded to the flames of fire licking him, and she stood for a while in dazed silence.

Suddenly, one of the *lamas* blew a horn made from a large sea-shell. The deafening and eerie sound was the signal for other family members in the village to bring grain offerings to throw over the stone heap. Then, all the mourners made straight for the village tap to purify themselves. Some of the male relatives who had not yet shaved their heads and eyebrows did so.

As memories of her uncle's death flooded back, Renu wondered what a Christian funeral would be like. By now, a sizeable crowd had gathered.

Contrary to her expectation her father's journey to the grave did not offend the rest of the village. In order to avoid all possible causes of friction, the Christians had decided not to use the hill top common to all other Tamangs. Rather they chose a plot of wasteland a little way downhill away from the village. Stray cattle grazed on it from time to time. Otherwise, villagers avoided it because it was believed to be haunted by demons.

Very soon Renu would see that the Christians did their funerals rather differently from what she had expected. As villagers watched, they hammered away at the coffin. Jogbir and his friends made it from planks taken from wooden boxes they had taken apart.

Meanwhile, Sanumaya tossed restlessly in her bed on the verandah. After she had regained consciousness in the early hours of the morning, her mourning had begun. Weeping with abandon, she cursed the police with one breath, *Ram* with another, pulled at her own hair, and repeatedly beat her chest.

'I told him not to go after *Yesu*,' she moaned deliriously. 'How right I was! The gods have had their revenge. They have finished my husband!' Renu tried to keep her quiet, but she too broke down only too frequently. After she could weep no more, she started helping Jogbir. She insisted on laying the sheet, which she had so carefully arranged on her father's bed, at the bottom of the coffin. Jogbir placed it so that the two sides would cover Mahila when they eventually brought him down. Soon they had placed him in. Wiping her sudden burst of tears away, Renu regretted that she had no time to wash the sheet. Jogbir hammered nails onto the cover at Mahila's head and feet to keep it in place.

There was no way Sanumaya would be persuaded to attend the funeral, but she allowed her daughter to go. Renu walked at Patrus' side as eight men carried the coffin. Suddenly, Sushila seemed to appear from nowhere and clasp her hand. Gangaram followed. Renu had seen such a crowd at Dhanee Gaon only once before, the day the villagers testified against the Christians. Downhill, the people extended, behind and in front of the coffin. Downhill, Mahila went as he had done on his two feet all his life; but that day for the last time. Renu looked ahead, and saw the freshly dug grave. Many had lain around that pit for generations, but her father would enter it as the first disciple of *Yesu*. Jogbir and friends rested the coffin gently on the fresh earth next to the grave, and lifted up the cover. Renu looked at her father's face. He radiates peace and dignity, she said to herself.

As Jogbir and his companions hammered more nails into the cover that hid Father's face from her forever, she rested her head on Sushila's shoulders and wept.

'Why has all this happened?' she asked. 'I did not harm anybody!' Sushila did not reply but just stroked Renu's hair gently. With the help of ropes, they gently lowered the coffin into the grave. Never would Father run downhill again.

CHAPTER
TWELVE

BRAVER THAN THE GURKHAS

For the funeral, Patrus had chosen a hymn which Renu suggested her father would have liked – the song about heaven. The Christians joined in. Hearing people singing on a mournful occasion, the villagers stood amazed. Patrus opened his Bible, and faced the crowd. 'A short verse from the Book of God, the Bible, 1 Corinthians, chapter 15, and verses 55 to 57: "Where, Death, is your victory? Where, Death, is your power to hurt? Death gets its power to hurt from sin, and sin gets its power from the Law. But thanks be to God who gives us the victory through our Lord *Yesu*."

'Brothers, sisters, and friends in Dhanee Gaon! We've done strange things today. We've gathered in great numbers to pay our last respects to a man who just a few months ago terrorised all of you with his drunken adventures. We've sung at his funeral when we are accustomed to see most other people mourn and weep. We've also read from this book.' Patrus shut the Bible, pointed to it, and opened it up again at his book mark.

'I must first explain to you that the Author of this book has made Mahila what he was the last two months. This book gives us the courage to sing, to sing about victory, to sing about heaven. The first verse I read emphasises death as the inevitable consequence of sin. We have to die because we've sinned. The body that has sinned cannot face God. It has to perish. However, verse 57 tells us that death doesn't have the last word for someone who has trusted in *Yesu*. *Yesu* paid the greatest penalty ever demanded. *Yesu*, the sinless incarnation of God, died for our sins. We can compare His death with the bail Pastor Gangaram and I have paid to remain out of prison.' Patrus looked gently at Gangaram who stared straight ahead.

'But *Yesu*'s sacrifice is more than bail. It is the final victory over the enemy – eternal death. Those who trust in *Yesu* have this victory over death as a gift. So, a verse we didn't read, verse 53 in the same chapter says: "For this perishable body must put on the imperishable, and this mortal body must put on immortality." What does the writer mean here? We can understand this best by examining what *Yesu* Himself has done. He died a terrible death on the cross. His disciples placed His body in a borrowed tomb. On the third day, some disciples went to look for the corpse. They didn't find it. He had risen from the dead. He had taken a new body, a body that walls or barriers couldn't hinder. He appeared to Thomas and the other disciples in a room completely closed.

'Because Mahila trusted in *Yesu*, I believe *Yesu* has already given him a body like His own. Not the sinful, emaciated, disease-infested body which we'll bury in a few minutes; but the glorious immortal body. Did the disciples recognise *Yesu* in His new resurrected body? Yes, they did. *Yesu* even had the holes which the nails made in His hands. Will Renu recognise her father? Yes, she will. Except, her father won't suffer from torture and disease as he did here. He can't because *Yesu* has given him a new body.

'That explains why Christians sing at funerals. Christians know that their beloved friend has already received this new body. He or she who has departed from them enjoys eternal friendship with *Yesu*. Of course, any separation causes agony. We'll miss Mahila severely in our church, in our village; but we rejoice that his pain has ceased.

'We can describe this occasion today by one word – "first". I've had the privilege of conducting the first funeral in this lovely village where I've spent four years of my life. This year may well be my last. Yesterday, the court gave me one week to pack up, and leave. My constant pleading extended the time to a month. By then my family and I'll have to go. The *Muluki Ain* prescribes it. The law regards me a foreigner. I can't deny it. I come from Darjeeling, and have Indian citizenship. So I count this funeral a privilege. It is like the first seed you farmers sow. It will surely bear fruit later on.

'However, I want to apply the term "first" to Mahila himself. I've heard of police atrocities to Christians in many places all over the country. Sometimes, they broke sticks on the bare backs of our brothers. Sometimes, they marched them hungry for days. In some cases, they forced them to bow down to stone idols. At times, they beat them close to death. However, our Lord considered Mahila worthy of martyrdom. He stands head and shoulders above us. The Nepali church has just produced her first martyr. We pay our respects to him.

'After the first week of torture, Mahila felt well enough to talk. He described the agonies he went through, but said that he had no grudges against the police. In fact he said he would tell them of the love of *Yesu* as soon as he could walk again. That day never came. However, what he said reminds me of verse 58 – "So then, my dear brothers and sisters, stand firm and steady. Keep busy always in your work for the Lord, since you know that nothing you do in the Lord's service is ever useless."

'Even till his last wakeful moment, Mahila was faithful to his Lord. Mahila leaves us this message of reconciliation. No grudges, please, against the police who have arrested us. No revenge, for the Bible says vengeance belongs to the Lord. Rather we should pray for them and the higher authorities who have made such unjust laws, laws that degrade our beloved country in the eyes of the world. Mahila has proved himself an example of supreme forgiveness, and unconditional love, even to those who tormented him. Could he speak to us now, I'm sure the first part of verse 58 would aptly summarise what he'd like to say to us: "So then, my dear brothers and sisters, stand firm and steady." ' Patrus shut his Bible, and stared harder at the audience.

'Mahila liked telling me stories of the battles he fought in Burma during World War II. Those battles, there and elsewhere, made the Gurkha soldiers world famous. Many legends have grown about them, and we rightly feel proud of their bravery. However, in Mahila, I've seen one much braver. During his last months, Mahila didn't fight for a government, but for the Lord who had sacrificed Himself to save you and me. Mahila didn't use guns and bullets, but suffering and patience. The Gurkhas fought for livelihood and medals, Mahila for love. Let's bow our heads to our Lord *Yesu* in gratitude for the life and testimony of Mahila, this great son of Dhanee Gaon, one braver than the Gurkhas!'

CHAPTER
THIRTEEN

NEVER ALONE

Trouble never comes alone, thought Renu, as she and Sanumaya walked away from the church after the Saturday service. Renu had stopped attending church and Sunday school ever since she had boarded the bus for the ill-fated trip to Darjeeling. After her father had come home beaten and bruised, she had all the more excuse not to go. She took courage the second Saturday after her father's burial, but only by coaxing her mother to come along. Sanumaya agreed just to avoid the monotony at home. Besides, the Christians had shown her a lot of sympathy, and she had overcome her original hostility towards them. She did not see any harm in observing how they worshipped. Renu decided that Patrus had already groomed Jogbir as his successor. While Patrus sat in the front taking notes on his student's performance in the 'pulpit', just an ordinary table, Jogbir would preach. As a farmer like anyone else in the village, Jogbir would make a living from his small plot of land. No one could accuse Jogbir of accepting *Yesu* because he received American money. No one would call him a 'foreigner's tail'. Jogbir, a son of the soil, would live by the soil. Even without the stigma of foreign money, he would have enough trouble leading the newly founded church of Dhanee Gaon.

However, news of Jogbir's friend Karna distressed Renu. Karna had decided to migrate to Lama Gahra. He had already sold his land and property to a resident of his new village. Patrus announced that Jogbir, he, and the church committee had pleaded with Karna not to go, but too late and in vain. Reluctantly, Patrus prayed for Karna, his wife Thuli, son Mangal, and daughter Sabita that they might go out as representatives of Christ to Lama Gahra. The church murmured prayers after him, but Renu found it terribly depressing.

They've expelled our pastor, he has expelled himself, thought Renu. She guessed his denial of *Yesu* after the arrest weighed heavily on him. *Yesu* had forgiven Karna. Karna had not forgiven himself.

Two more weeks remained for the pastor to care for the church in Dhanee Gaon. They would all miss him badly. On the other hand she remembered *Yesu's* promise, never to leave them alone.

Three-quarters of the way along the path after the church service, Renu turned pale and had to sit down on the ground.

'I feel sick,' she said to Mother who looked totally puzzled. Renu had hardly eaten anything before going to church. In the next second, Renu threw up the tea she had taken that morning, and wiped her mouth with the tip of her *fariah*.

'I've noticed your strange behaviour for some time now,' Sanumaya said. 'Tell me the truth, what's the matter?'

'I shall,' Renu said, 'but let's get home first.' Sanumaya supported Renu on her right arm, and slowly led her towards the verandah of their home. The shade made Renu feel a lot better. Mother gave her a jug of water to rinse her mouth.

'I'll tell you the truth,' Renu hesitated a bit. 'I . . . I am pregnant!'

'Pregnant!' Sanumaya covered her face, and almost screamed. 'I can't believe it. One thing after another!'

'I've lied to you all along,' Renu admitted. 'God pricked my conscience severely at church today. I'll tell you everything, but I have to tell the pastor and his wife too. Their son lured me to Darjeeling!'

'But you said you spent three nights in Kathmandu!' Sanumaya protested.

'I lied to you, I had to. I thought I'd get away with it. I didn't realise this would happen!'

'Oh, trouble never comes alone,' Sanumaya moaned.

'I've been thinking exactly the same,' answered Renu, and lay on the straw mat.

Renu heard Mother go in and make a curious but familiar noise from her throat.

Poor woman, thought Renu, she wants to drown her troubles by drinking as much water as she can. After a few seconds

Mother came out.

'The sun has made me terribly thirsty,' Sanumaya said, 'but I should go and call the pastor and his wife. Go up and lie on your bed.'

'Only they should come,' Renu begged, 'no one else please.'

She felt so tired she thought she would not make it to the top of the ladder. With her head spinning wildly, she crawled up; and having reached her bed, collapsed on top of it. Then she broke down and cried, not knowing how she would face the next few hours.

'Why have you treated me so, *Yesu*?' she asked. 'I'm sorry I disobeyed you. I'm paying for it dearly, don't you see?'

Scarcely half an hour had passed before Patrus, Esther, and her mother, sitting where Father once lay, faced her. Renu got up on her bed, and leaned against the wall on her pillow.

'We rushed here as soon as Sanumaya came to call us,' Esther took the initiative in breaking the silence, 'because last week we received a strange letter from Sudeep.' Esther looked at her husband who took the crumpled aerogramme from his shirt pocket.

'What did he say?' asked Renu.

'Well, we know our son has his ups and downs in his Christian life. So we don't go by all that he writes. He told us not to believe a word you say. He said you wanted to see Darjeeling so much that he had to take you.'

'I have acted as a child, very foolishly,' Renu admitted. 'I ask forgiveness from you and from the Lord *Yesu*. I take full blame. Sudeep promised to marry me, to send me to school. I wanted to train as a nurse. I wanted to escape the drudgery of village life. I fully trusted Sudeep, even to the extent of eloping with him while my father was still in police custody. I should have been content to stay where God has placed me. That's where I've gone wrong.'

'Did you make it to Darjeeling then?' Patrus broke in.

'No, I returned from the border at Kakervitta.'

'What happened?'

'Sudeep left me!' Renu started to sob. 'In the bus we heard two people in front of us talking of strange events. The police had just arrested people who took girls across the border to sell them in India. In fact one had a newspaper that told of the recent arrests they had made at Kakervitta. Both of us heard it. I saw Sudeep turn pale. He must have feared being suspected of taking me for the same purpose. He hardly talked after that ... A man at the border checked his baggage, and took quite a while to check mine. He went through each item in my bag to see if I'd hidden something. When he'd finished checking it, I looked for Sudeep, but couldn't find him. At last I saw him speeding off in an auto-rickshaw. I stood rooted to the spot, and cried. The man who checked my bag and a policeman took me away.'

'But I can't understand how you've become pregnant,' broke in Esther, sounding very protective over her son. 'Sanumaya told me of your symptoms lately.'

'Yes,' wept Renu. 'Please don't worry, Sudeep didn't do it. We travelled in buses day and night.'

'Who did it then?' Patrus showed impatience as the suspense dragged on.

'A policeman! How well I remember the number of his shoulder badge: 342414!' Renu broke down into an uncontrollable sob. Her mother joined her. Patrus shook his head slowly from side to side. Esther stared into the space in front of her, trying to take in what she had just heard, trying to determine how far her son was to blame.

'Didn't you fight back, yell or scream?' Patrus asked sadly.

'They kept me sitting on a bench the whole of that day,' said Renu, wiping her eyes and nose. 'Towards seven at night two men and a policewoman took me to the office and asked questions. The man sitting behind the desk saw the book I had, and concluded I was a Christian. He said he knew about Christians. They plagued society like leeches. He would exterminate them if he could.' Renu started sobbing again.

'After about two hours everyone left the room. I sat alone trembling. Then the man who sat behind the desk returned on his own. He shut the door first then turned off the electric light. As I screamed, he gagged my mouth. He said he had never slept with a Christian girl before ... The next day, the same man warned me to keep quiet about it. Towards the evening, he persuaded a bus driver that I was his relative; and, without even buying a ticket, sent me off. I travelled free to Kathmandu.' Through her tears, Renu saw them all looking aghast.

176

After some uneasiness, Patrus broke the silence. 'Please forgive us for what our son has done to you. We'd have celebrated if he had married you, even after this elopement. We'd have considered him fortunate to have a wife like you. The rascal! He's murdered us by his behaviour. Our Lord knew it. No wonder the judge in Trisuli has expelled us from the country.' Renu stared at Patrus.

'Many Christians over there are so in name only. They don't really know the Lord. My son is no exception,' Esther added. 'At least the persecution here keeps Christians more dedicated.'

'Esther, promise me you'll keep this matter entirely quiet,' Patrus warned his wife. 'Don't even tell Sushila. Renu has asked to be forgiven for her foolishness. We can't hold her responsible for the pregnancy; neither will God.'

'Forgive our son, forgive the policeman,' Esther pleaded with Renu. 'You can't grow in the Christian life unless you do. I believe the Lord will work everything out for your good somehow. Keep on trusting in Him.'

'Yes, Renu, all this has made us even closer to you. From now on, I'll consider you my second daughter. I can't stay here, but I'll write . . .' Patrus broke down. His wife handed him a handkerchief from her bag.

'Remember Darjeeling and us not for what my son has done to you, but for what we've tried to do. No one's perfect – we've failed as far as our son is concerned; but we did bring *Yesu* to you.'

Also the jackass called Sudeep! Renu thought to herself.

'Pray to Him daily. He will prove a better friend than we ever can be, a better father than Mahila ever was . . .' Patrus cried again.

Renu nodded her head in agreement. Suddenly, she felt her tears dry up. She tried to smile.

'We should commit all this to the Lord in prayer,' said Esther looking at her husband. '*Rajah*, why don't you pray. We've spent quite a lot of time here already. Sushila may suspect something's wrong. We'd better go home.' Renu couldn't focus on what Patrus prayed. Her body still felt strange. She put on a faint smile as the pastor and his wife left.

177

***

Mother lay snoring. Renu calculated the time was close to midnight. She tried not to wake up Mother, but she wondered if she could hold on.

'Mother,' she moaned, 'Mother.'

'Hmm!' responded Sanumaya.

'I don't know what's happening to me,' Renu moaned. 'I may die.'

Suddenly, Sanumaya's bed creaked all over. Renu heard her mother fumbling for matches. Sanumaya lighted the kerosine lamp.

'What's the matter?'

'There's a piercing pain in my stomach,' Renu replied. 'It's more frequent now. I thought it would go away, but it didn't.' Sanumaya laid her right hand on Renu's stomach. She felt Renu's bed.

'Blood,' she shrieked, looking at her hand in the pale yellow light.

'I have been bleeding like this for some time. My stomach's churning up. Oh, the pain's much worse!' Renu curled up, and her face beaded with sweat.

'I know now,' exclaimed Sanumaya. 'Miscarriage, *Ram, Ram,* miscarriage! You're every inch my daughter, even to the point of having miscarriages! I've had four events like this. With me it happened only much later, in the fifth or the sixth month . . . Keep your legs apart, Renu. Take deep breaths!'

Renu saw her mother take full control. She folded a tattered bed sheet, and put it under Renu. 'I'll light the fire and heat some water,' Sanumaya said. Renu heard her mother rush downstairs.

Renu's pain became more intense and rapid. Taking deep breaths, she soon got into a rhythm that made it more bearable. Then she screamed as if a tiger was chasing her! At that moment, it was over. Mother's footsteps sounded on the ladder.

'The pain's gone,' Renu said. 'Thank God, the pain's gone.'

'What?' exclaimed Sanumaya, turning away the quilt from Renu's leg. 'Over already . . . oh, what a mess!' Sanumaya pulled the sheet away, and carefully folded it all up.

'Hold on,' she said. 'I'd better bury it before dawn.' Renu suddenly felt ten years younger.

Sanumaya must have been away fifteen minutes. She came with a bowl of steaming water in one hand, and a cup in the other. 'Drink this black tea. I can't milk the cow now!'

'You've made it so sweet!' fussed Renu, leaning against the wall and taking quick hungry sips.

'My *nani*,' Sanumaya sounded excited. 'You acted foolishly, but your God has given you another chance. Now you can build a new life.' Sanumaya started wiping the sweat off Renu's face.

'I shall,' Renu replied. 'I'll finish my high school studies first. Then I'll train as a nurse.'

'How will you do that?' asked Sanumaya. 'Oh, yes, I'll still get Father's pension. I'll help you as much as I can.'

'No, Mother, you'll need that money at home . . . On the night Father passed away, Pastor Gangaram talked to me. He said he'd ask his church to give me a scholarship to complete high school. After I pass, he promised to help me get a place to train as a nurse in Kathmandu. If I don't get a place in the hostel, I can even live in his home, and go to college each day. God had such wonderful plans for me. I acted stupidly to run away with such a fellow.'

'How will all that help me? You'll marry and go away.'

'Marry? Never! Not after what men have done to me,' answered Renu. 'After my training, I'll work some years in Kathmandu to save money. You can live with me there if you like. Then I'll open a small clinic in Dhanee Gaon, right in this house. No more walking three hours to get medicine!'

'My *nani*, don't talk so loudly,' said Sanumaya, wiping Renu's thighs with a wet, steaming cloth. 'The dogs in the village may start barking.' Sanumaya went to the ground floor to throw the dirty water away.

'Mother,' called Renu when the ladder creaked again.

'We should go to sleep soon. You need to rest as much as you can. What?'

'You should tell the pastor and his wife what has just happened.'

'I've already thought of that,' Sanumaya replied. 'This'll bring peace to their hearts again. They could scarcely believe what their son had done to you, leaving you in the lurch . . . This will bring peace to my heart too. I used to regret that none of my sons have lived to take care of me. No more! Now, I can look forward to old age. You may bring more glory to Dhanee Gaon than any son could. Besides, now I'll never be alone! '

CHAPTER
FOURTEEN

INSPIRATION

Mother was crying. Only Renu knew the reason! Sanumaya had become too attached to Esther. Renu knew it was one-sided love. Esther had not visited them after they had discussed Renu's pregnancy. But a departure was no occasion to keep grudges, and Renu had accompanied her mother to see the Masih family off. On the courtyard of the house Patrus and family had rented for the last four years stood six *dokos* full of suitcases, bags, bedding, utensils, and books. Christians and other villagers had gathered at the wall to witness the event. While Sanumaya quietly wiped her tears away from her cheeks, Renu sat speechless on the verandah. Esther went in and out, sometimes giving orders to the porters, sometimes to her daughter Sushila. Jogbir, useful as always, had hired the right porters. He wanted to make sure the pastor and his family caught the noon bus to Kathmandu. Missing it would mean an extra night in Trisuli instead of the warm hospitality of Pastor Gangaram. As Jogbir ran about to make sure they left Dhanee Gaon by eight that morning, Renu silently wished the contingent would not leave at all.

'Renu!' Sushila called. 'My father wants to see you.' Renu left her mother on the verandah, and went inside. The table in the kitchen had a dismal look about it. The cupboards were empty. The pastor had decided to leave the furniture for his kind non-Christian landlord. As Renu stood uneasily, Jogbir entered.

'Let's sit down and talk for few minutes,' Patrus, offering a chair, said to Jogbir. 'Some days ago Renu wanted me to baptise her. I've prayed about it till now. We love Renu as our daughter. I would have counted it a great privilege to baptise her before I left. However, I didn't want to do anything rashly.'

He's afraid he will be arrested again, thought Renu.

'Besides, I didn't have any time for the baptismal lessons.' Patrus looked at Renu, then at Jogbir.

'Jogbir *bhai*, I believe you should give her the baptismal classes, and then the baptism. Choose the water pond more carefully this time!' Patrus had a twinkle in his eye. Jogbir blushed. Renu guessed Patrus referred to her father's ill-fated 'Jordan experience', and felt furious.

How can he joke about it? she thought and controlled herself.

'You could just ask one of the committee members to help you in the water. Do it with much prayer. ' Jogbir nodded in agreement.

'We've seen God's hands guide you and protect you in amazing ways.' Patrus assured Renu. 'Remember the example of your father. Send me a letter the day after your baptism. Pray for me and *pastorni ama* at least a minute a day. I'll keep in touch through letters. Like your father, aim to be braver than the Gurkhas! I'll pray for you.' Spontaneously, Patrus shut his eyes in prayer. At the 'amen', Esther stood by his side.

'*Rajah*,' she said. 'I can walk, but only slowly. We ought to leave.' Just then Sushila appeared, and embraced Renu.

'Wait!' Sushila pleaded just as quickly and ran off leaving Renu puzzled. A few seconds later, Sushila appeared with an object that Renu could well have done without. 'I brought this for you,' Sushila said. 'I couldn't think of a better parting gift. This will remind you of the wonderful times we had at Sunday school.' Renu looked at Sudeep's guitar in dismay.

'Oh, Sushila!' Esther reprimanded with disapproval.

'I'll take it all the same,' Renu replied quickly to ease the situation.

'Sudeep wore out the cardboard case, but you can sew a pretty cloth cover,' Sushila suggested. 'Here, take this sheet to keep it in for now!' Renu folded the bed sheet, covered the guitar, and held the instrument by its neck.

'I have one last request to make,' Renu said, looking at Esther. 'Please hug my mother before you leave. Remembering your kindness, she's crying on the verandah.'

'Bless her. I surely shall, Renu. I'll not forget . . . We ought to pray and leave.'

She's surely in a hurry to leave, thought Renu.

This time, out in the courtyard, Jogbir prayed. He rambled on, almost reciting the whole history of the last four years. At last he came to the point when he concentrated on safety for the bus journey, that the nuts and bolts on the vehicle would not turn loose, that the driver would not fall asleep or get drunk. Immediately, after the 'amen' he looked at his watch. 'We ought to have left long ago!' Jogbir exclaimed.

Esther approached Sanumaya. Rather awkwardly, the educated graduate from Darjeeling embraced the rustic illiterate of Dhanee Gaon. 'I'll pray for you,' Esther, surprised that she had lost control over herself, mumbled in a broken voice. Sanumaya folded her palms in a *namasthe*, the symbol which meant so much more than thanks.

Together with a few others, Renu watched. The porters left first. Jogbir followed them as if to keep guard, then Esther, then Patrus, then Sushila. Renu's eyes followed the trail downhill to the bend in the path. Finally, Sushila waved to her for the last time; and disappeared. Renu dropped her head on Sanumaya's shoulder.

After most of the Christians had dispersed, Renu looked longingly once more at the door she had just come out of a few minutes before. She almost expected Sushila to emerge, and embrace her again. Although neither she nor her mother felt like eating much that day, Renu beckoned her to go home and start the fire for the morning meal. Sanumaya noticed a large object Renu held, hidden in the sheet. 'Sushila gave this as a parting gift, in total innocence,' Renu said. 'I accepted it.' Renu lifted up the cloth a bit, and revealed the guitar underneath.

'What will you do with it?' asked Sanumaya.

'Soon, you'll know,' replied Renu. 'I want to get to the cliff and have one last glimpse of Sushila. Let's go.'

Sanumaya and Renu ran alongside their home towards the cliff. The *Pradhan Panch* lived close by, but neither thought of him just then. They wanted to see the contingent going down the hill. Both Renu and her mother had miscalculated. The cliff did not offer any view of the path down to the Trisuli. The dense, shrubby forest completely hid the dusty track. Both sat close to the cliff, straining their eyes. Renu stood up.

'Sit down, Renu,' her mother warned her. 'You may fall! I'm

afraid to go near the edge ever since I came here to throw myself over.'

'Then, let this go over!' replied Renu. All of a sudden, Sanumaya saw the guitar fly above her head.

'Renu, what have you done? You foolish girl, what have you done?'

'I had to do it, Mother!' Renu shouted back, 'I feel much better now, much better.' As if thoroughly exhausted, Renu sat down, and rested her chin on her right palm. Sanumaya crept towards the edge.

'You've shattered it,' Sanumaya reported to Renu. 'It'll never make music now!'

'Nor will its previous owner,' replied Renu, not bothering to look over the cliff. 'Let's go home and get on with our work.'

LASTLY . . .

Things change in five years, and they have changed as much for Renu as for everybody else. Pastor Gangaram kept his promise to her. Helping Mother with the cattle and farming morning and evening, Renu attended school during the day; and studied late into the night by the flicker of her kerosine lamp. People in Trisuli bazaar marvelled at her School Leaving Certificate result, a first division pass for the first time in the district. This enabled her to win a place in the nursing school without any of the string pulling which Gangaram detested so much.

In spite of his habit of rambling while preaching, Jogbir turned into a good pastor after all. His eagerness to do anything to help soon won the heart of the congregation. Many baptisms followed after the first – Renu's. Recently, he has a newcomer in the audience, the former *Pradhan Panch*. After he lost the elections, the *Pradhan Panch* had no qualms about sitting through the Saturday church worship. Seeing some ex-lepers in the congregation, the former 'king of the village' started treating his first wife Phulmati better. For Jogbir this incident was a sermon in itself: power corrupts, and loss of it can at times have salutary effects!

The loneliness Sanumaya feared she would encounter during old age never occurred. Two years ago, she too accepted baptism. At once, she had a family: village-wide, nation-wide, and, though she cannot understand it, world-wide. She does not like to miss a single prayer meeting or a Bible study. Once she went to Kathmandu to spend a weekend with Renu in Pastor Gangaram's church, but discovered no city can replace Dhanee Gaon. Soon, she pestered her daughter to put her on a bus going back home! Now she longs for

Renu to finish her training, and establish a private clinic in her own village.

After one year of faithfully going to court in Trisuli on the appointed dates (and of course, keeping his preaching appointments in Dhanee Gaon!), Pastor Gangaram received a seven-year sentence: one year for converting himself to *Yesu*, six years for baptising Mahila. Since the *Muluki Ain* would require him to renounce his faith in *Yesu* even after spending seven years in jail, his Hindu, but democratic, lawyer has advised him to fight on right up to the Supreme Court.

The non-Christians fared better than Gangaram. Not surprisingly, the district court found the two men and the woman, tortured to confession, guilty. The regional court acquitted them! I shudder to think of the scars which all three, especially the woman, must bear. Can they ever adjust to normal living again?

Karna did not fit well into the surroundings and the church of Lama Gahra. I hear he wants either to return to Dhanee Gaon or to leave Nepal altogether for the religious liberty of India. I sympathise with him. Recently, the government has raised the bail to Rs 9125 per year, a colossal jump from Rs 540, and an impossible figure when we consider that an average worker earns about Rs 500 per month. However, I would advise Karna and others wanting to avoid persecution to sit still. They say, the best way is always *through!*

Finally, Mahila! He does not live yet he lives on. Doctors I have consulted generally agree with the diagnosis of the health assistant. Some would suggest a multiple cause for the death – a mixture of kidney and brain haemorrhages, severe injuries, and the trauma he went through. Till facts emerge to the contrary, I believe Mahila had the rare privilege of witnessing to his Lord, through death. As the first Nepali Christian martyr, Mahila continues to inspire me. This book hardly qualifies as a tribute.

GLOSSARY

Ama Mother. Combined with *pastorni*, it forms a popular form of address for the pastor's wife.

Asthami The eighth day of the festival of *Dasain*.

Ba Father. It can be applied to one's own father or some father-figure.

Babu An affectionate term used by an elderly person for someone younger, usually a boy.

Bahini Younger sister. A term used also to address a younger girl or woman.

Baisakh The first month, starting mid-April, in the Nepali calendar.

Bhai Younger brother. A term used to address a boy or a younger man.

Bishnu The main sustainer god in the Hindu religion.

Brahmin The priestly caste of the Hindus. Strict Brahmins do not use vessels utilised by those of the 'low caste', to which Christians are usually relegated.

CDO The Chief District Officer, the administrative head of a district.

Dahl A thick soup of lentils.

Dai Elder brother. A term used to address an elder man.

Dasain The major Hindu festival usually falling at the end of September and the beginning of October. It normally lasts ten days, and involves a lot of animal sacrifices on the eighth.

Dhindo Basic food of the poor in villages. Corn or wheat flour is added to boiling water. The paste is stirred till it hardens.

Didi Elder sister. Also a term of respect for an elder girl or woman.

Doko	A bamboo basket about three feet tall, broad at the top and narrow at the bottom. It is carried on the back. A rope around it and resting on the forehead of the porter keeps it in position.
Falgun	The Nepali month that starts from mid-February.
Fariah	Cheap cotton garment like the *sari*, but less dignified.
Gainda	The name of one brand of cigarettes produced in Nepal.
Guru	Teacher.
IGP	Inspector General of Police.
Jain	An adherent of Jainism which, in one of its tenets, prohibits the killing of any animal or insect.
Jai Masih	The Nepali equivalent of 'Glory to the Saviour,' a common Christian greeting.
Jestha	Second month, starting mid-May, in the Nepali year.
ji	The suffix added to any name to denote respect.
Krishna	Another deified Indian hero. Krishna is famous for his youthful pranks.
Kukri	The 'Gurkha knife.' The scythe-type of implement used for domestic work as well as warfare.
Lama	A Buddhist village priest who may make use of some folk medicine and charms to heal or (as is believed) change the behaviour of people.
Madal	An indigenous drum consisting of leather stretched on two sides of a wooden barrel approximately six inches in diameter and fourteen inches in length.
Muluki Ain	The legal code, a 'Bible' for the law courts in Nepal. It has not been translated into English, and so remains hidden from the eyes of the world. Part 4, chapter 19, section 1 of the *Muluki Ain* runs as follows:

        'No person shall propagate Christianity, Islam or any other faith so as to disturb the traditional religion of the Hindu community in Nepal or to convert any adherent of the Hindu religion to these faiths. Anyone attempting to do so shall be imprisoned for three years; where conversion has been effected, for six years; if by a foreign citizen, he shall, in addition, be expelled from the country. Any Hindu who converts himself into any of the above-mentioned religions shall be imprisoned for a maximum period of one year. For just an attempt to convert himself, he shall be fined Rs. 100. In case conversion has already been effected, it shall be invalidated, and such a person shall remain in his Hindu religion.'

Namasthe	A symbol, of greetings or thanks, consisting of palms joined and raised chest high.
Nani	Term of affection used by elderly person for younger ones, usually girls.
Patrus *Masih*	*Patrus* is the Nepali equivalent for 'Peter'; *Masih*, a common surname meaning 'Christian'.
Pradhan *Panch*	The village administrator elected for a period of five years.
Pastorni	The pastor's wife.
Puri	Thin chapaties (bread, like pancakes) fried in mustard oil.
Ram	The ancient king of Ayodhya, India. Deified, he is worshipped widely in India and Nepal.
Rajah	Literally 'king', a term some wives employ for their husbands.
Rana	The *de facto* rulers of Nepal for 104 years prior to 1950 AD. The king was just a figure-head then. The 'Rana rule' has become a symbol of isolation and oppression.
Subbha	A junior civilian officer akin to the head clerk.
Two *Thousand* *and* *Seven* (2007)	1950 AD. The revolution that year gave Nepal a secular constitution similar to that of modern India. That was suspended in 1960.
Yesu	Jesus.

189

Even false Xns get persecuted.

For further details of Word products please complete coupon below.

Books ☐

Word Records – Cassettes ☐

Lifelifter Cassettes ☐

Video ☐

Please tick items of interest

Name..

Address..

....

....

Word Publishing
Word (UK) Ltd
9 Holdom Avenue, Bletchley, Milton Keynes.
MK1 1QU